TANGLED WEB

TANGLED WEB

Eunice Wilkie

Oh, what a tangled web we weave,
When first we practise to deceive!

Sir Walter Scott, 1808

TANGLED WEB
EUNICE WILKIE

Written & illustrated by Eunice Wilkie
www.aletheiabooks.co
Copyright © 2021

This book is also available as an ebook and audio book.
For more information, please visit

www.aletheiabooks.co

Acknowledgement

*I would like to thank Ruth Chesney and Sean Watt for their
invaluable comments and suggestions which helped to shape and
improve this story. The support and reassurance of such friends is
greatly appreciated; it was undoubtedly vital to the completion
and publication of this book. Thank you very much!*

RITCHIE
John Ritchie Publishing

40 Beansburn, Kilmarnock, Scotland
www.ritchiechristianmedia.co.uk

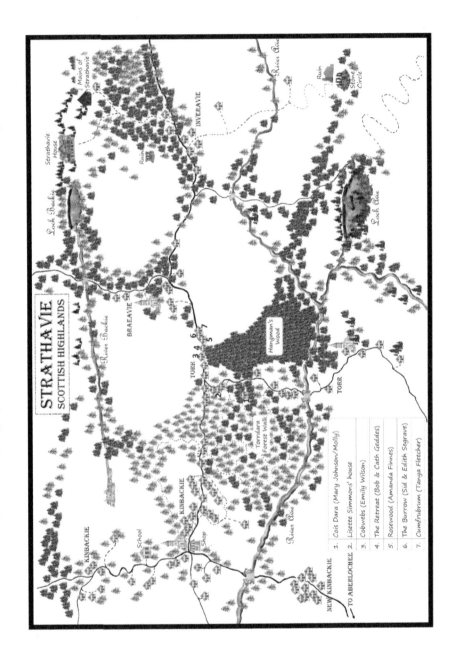

STRATHAVIE
SCOTTISH HIGHLANDS

Mains of Strathavie

Strathavie House

Loch Backie

River Backie

BRAEAVIE

River Pine

Ruin

Loch Pine

INVERAVIE

Ruin

Stone Circle

Torrdara Forest Walk

Hangman's Wood

TORR 3 4 6

5 7

2

1

TORR

KINBACKIE

School

Shop

River Pine

KINBACKIE

NEW KINBACKIE

TO ABERLOCHEE

1. Cois Dara (Mary Johnson/Molly)
2. Lisette Simmons' house
3. Cobwebs (Emily Wilson)
4. The Retreat (Bob & Cath Geddes)
5. Rosewood (Amanda Finnies)
6. The Burrow (Sid & Edith Segrave)
7. Cwmfrubrum (Tanya Fletcher)

4

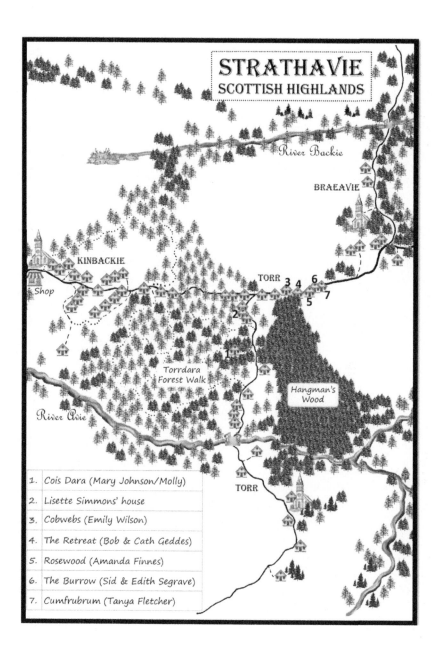

STRATHAVIE
SCOTTISH HIGHLANDS

River Backie

BRAEAVIE

KINBACKIE

Shop

TORR 3 4 6
5 7
2

1

Torrdara
Forest Walk

Hangman's
Wood

River Avie

TORR

1.	Cois Dara (Mary Johnson/Molly)
2.	Lisette Simmons' house
3.	Cobwebs (Emily Wilson)
4.	The Retreat (Bob & Cath Geddes)
5.	Rosewood (Amanda Finnes)
6.	The Burrow (Sid & Edith Segrave)
7.	Cumfrubrum (Tanya Fletcher)

CHAPTER 1

"Molly's dead."

Cath stared at Lisette. "*Dead?*"

Amanda shook her head. "She was well over eighty, after all."

Lisette nodded. "Exactly. Just one of those things. Nothing suspicious about it, nothing to worry about."

"*Nothing to worry about?!*" Cath looked wildly at her two neighbours. At Amanda, sitting hunched forward in her deckchair, swirling dregs of tea around in her mug and watching her small, fat dog, Faroe, who was looking longingly through the fence at the happy melee of Lisette and Cath's two far larger canines. As for Lisette, while Cath preferred her brashness to Amanda's feeble wavering, there was a recklessness about Lisette which was unsettling.

"In case you've forgotten, *Molly's money* is in *my* garage!" Cath hissed fiercely. She glanced over her shoulder at her own back garden, a few metres from the field in which she stood. She did *not* want her husband, Bob, to overhear. His involvement was the last thing this situation needed. "You should just put it back!" But even as she said it, Cath wasn't sure she believed it. *Replace the money? When no one, apart from them, might know it was missing?*

"I could take the briefcase–" began Lisette, and then stopped abruptly. She was looking past Amanda's small bungalow to the two houses at the end of the row. Between Amanda's house and the final two, you could glimpse the narrow road and any passing traffic.

"What is it?" Amanda sat up abruptly.

"Police!"

They didn't stay. Despite Lisette's reassurance that they weren't doing any wrong – just three neighbours meeting for a socially distanced evening chat during lockdown – the sudden presence of the police was surprisingly disconcerting. They agreed to discuss the matter the following evening. Cath would look after the cash for another night.

Slowly, Cath lifted the latch on her back garden gate. She had more time to decide what to do. *As long as Bob didn't find the money.*

***

Sid and Edith Segrave had lived in *The Burrow* for thirty-five years. They had moved to the tiny settlement of Torr in Strathavie when Sid's job with the Forestry Commission relocated them to the Scottish Highlands. They enjoyed their home and community. Sid was an elder in the church; Edith was a friend to all.

Latterly, they didn't know so many people in the strath. In the past twenty years, new houses had been built and incomers had flooded the beautiful glen. You could no longer visit the local shop in neighbouring Kinbackie and know everyone you met – although that didn't dissuade Elspeth, who ran the shop, from assigning names to every customer just in case she *ought* to know them.

Sid and Edith no longer knew their own direct neighbours. As Edith kept reminding Sid, the lady on their northern boundary was called Amanda. Edith had discovered her name and sent her a Christmas card. They had received a *'Seasons Greetings from Amanda'* card in return, which served the purpose of proving that Edith had the right name. They couldn't see Amanda's home through the thick shrubs that grew so prolifically on her border;

since lockdown they hadn't heard her come and go to work. Since they were 'shielding' from Covid, they couldn't go out at all.

Adjoining their compact single-storey home was a mirror image cottage. Another single lady lived there. Edith thought her name was Terri, but Sid thought she'd probably heard wrong. The truth didn't matter much; they never saw her, seldom heard her, sometimes doubted that she lived there at all.

But this evening, Edith once more mentioned the smell. "You remember I said about it yesterday, or the day before? Yes, Sid, I did! Are you *sure* you can't smell anything? It's a bit worrying, I think it's got worse."

"What's worrying about a smell?" asked Sid.

"It's the *type* of smell, that's worrying, like…"

"Well, like what?"

"I might as well come out with it – it smells like something is *dead!*"

Edith was not generally prone to dramatics, nor had she ever exhibited an extra-sensitive sense of smell. There were Covid symptoms that were to do with smells, weren't there? *Had they caught the virus after all?*

"*Where* did you smell it?"

"When we had the window open, the last couple of nights that have been so warm and fine."

Sid rolled his eyes. Edith never answered a direct question with a direct answer. "I said *where*, not *when!*"

"It's next door, Terri's, you know? Come and stand at the window, no, let's go outside. You'll soon see - or *smell* I should say! – what I mean…"

He laid down his crossword puzzle and shuffled after Edith. Out in the lovely spring evening Sid could hear the cuckoo call. He could hear neighbour's voices – women's voices, which were now often heard in the evening. He couldn't hear what they were saying, he didn't know who they were, but he enjoyed the fact that neighbours were being neighbourly, the way things ought to be.

Edith was by Terri's boundary fence – if that really was their neighbour's name. Untamed fir trees sprouted in all directions, hiding her garden. But through the greenery you could make out the bungalow. All the blinds and curtains were shut. One window was open, however, and when the curtain moved in the evening breeze … the smell! A sudden stench of decaying flesh, of death – just like Edith said! A dead animal was the most obvious explanation, but it was beyond Sid's ability to climb the fence, and beyond his desire to explore his unknown neighbour's property.

They returned to the house and Edith made them their evening drink. Ovaltine for her, hot milk for him. Sid had been thinking. He knew who to contact for advice. "I'll just phone young Ian."

He sipped his milk and tried to imagine an innocent explanation for the smell next door. But deep down he knew something was *wrong*.

CHAPTER 2

Detective Sergeant Ian Prentice touched the 'end' button on the phone call and rocked back in his office chair. It was well gone eight o'clock in the evening and the station was almost empty. Not unusually, he was going to be among the last to leave. Colleagues would have called Ian a high-flyer; not quite thirty, he was awaiting appointment to the post of Inspector in CID. Acquaintances thought him pleasant but reserved; friends knew him as adventurous and humorous – with a wickedly dry wit.

His unexpected evening phone call was from 'Uncle Sid'. Sid Segrave was not Ian's uncle any more than 'Aunt Edith' was his aunt. Sid was, in fact, his Sunday School teacher of many years past and was labelled 'uncle' because Ian's parents felt such a distinction between generations was respectful. Uncle Sid and Aunt Edith still sent Ian a birthday card and enthusiastically followed every detail of his life they could discover.

Ian knew Strathavie well. His parents lived in New Kinbackie, and Ian had attended the quaint rural school in Kinbackie during his early years. Normally speaking, his acquaintance with the rugged terrain outside of town wasn't an asset in law enforcement. But some weeks ago, he had been assigned an unusual case – mostly as a compliment to his acumen, but partly because of this local connection. It was a case referred from no less than the UK's National Crime Agency – the organisation that investigated serious and organised crime; or, as some thought of it, the UK's equivalent of the FBI.

It was a curious coincidence that Uncle Sid had phoned. Of course, the Segraves had no idea that Ian had a particular interest in Strathavie just now, and he didn't take Sid's report about *"something dead"* too seriously. Most likely a larger animal – maybe a deer – had died close by. But he drove out to Torr anyway – partly to reassure them, partly because of his *other case*.

In February 2020, just prior to lockdown, a large sum of money linked to a European-based drug cartel, had been traced through a GPS tracker the police had hacked to the unlikely, and vague, location of Strathavie. At which point the tracker was destroyed or disabled. The initial curiosity aroused by a case from the NCA – which was rare enough in the far north of the UK – was quickly replaced by the reality that all the Agency required from the local police was any information relating to Strathavie. The movements of local criminals, incidents, accidents, and such. The local police force was simply meant to be extra eyes and ears. Ian requested all intel on Strathavie, no matter how trivial, to be copied to him.

If the local police *had* been asked to proactively investigate, there was precious little they could do. Even without the raging coronavirus pandemic, a search of the hills, lochs, moorland and homes of Strathavie was completely impractical. The one thing in favour of discovering the missing cash was that Covid had hampered the movement of people (and therefore goods) around the country at roughly the same time as it had vanished. It was possible it was still concealed somewhere in the strath.

The journey to Torr involved ten miles on narrow roads and an ascent from the town of Aberlochee of about three hundred metres. Once through New Kinbackie (Ian's childhood home and where he hoped to beg a meal from his parents on his return), the road increased in gradient until it plateaued in Kinbackie, the first and largest of the mini settlements in Strathavie. Kinbackie contained the shop, school, and village hall. Other tiny settlements were individually named – Torr, Braeavie, Inveravie – but most folk no longer knew where one hamlet started and another ended. The only choice in amenities up and down the strath was in the selection of local churches – of mostly ancient lineage and now dwindling and closing one by one.

The sun was setting as he reached Sid and Edith's cottage. Mist was folding around the contours of the hills and the night promised frost by morning. There was no response from the Segrave's neighbour, but when Ian walked into the wilderness garden at the back of the house a breeze ruffled a curtain at an open window, and the stench was sudden and overwhelming.

The last light was fleeing the sky as Ian placed a call for police backup. Apart from the expertise of a pathologist, no medical assistance was required. The woman inside the house was far beyond help.

She had been dead for some time.

CHAPTER 3

Wednesday 29 April 2020

Ian dutifully reported the 'suspicious death' in Torr to Tracey Redding, their NCA contact in London. It was unusual for a woman in her forties to die alone at home, but it was still a stretch to believe it was somehow connected to the NCA case. However, since the local police force were investigating this unexplained death, Ian began more active digging around on anything unusual in Strathavie. He double-checked complaints, police-recorded incidents and crime, the whereabouts of local ne'er-do-wells, and he ran a search for other local deaths.

The Statutory Register of Deaths in Scotland recorded several deaths in the past month in the postcode which also covered Strathavie. In Torr, one death was recorded. Namely:

Mary Annabel Johnson, born Mary Annabel Martin, 3 January 1932; female; occupation – housewife; married to Iain MacIntyre Johnson, 3 September 1951; Cause of death – coronary heart disease; Date of death – 27 April 2020; Place of death – Cois Dara, Torr, Parish of Strathavie.

There was nothing that warranted further investigation. An old lady had died at home, at the ripe old age of eighty-eight, of a common cause, quite within the realms of reasonable expectation.

He searched the police database for crimes recorded in the same area. Nothing since lockdown. There were a couple of notes on the system – recorded as '*unconfirmed reports*': a phone call claiming someone was breaking lockdown regulations by going out too often, and the report of a '*strange man*' loitering close to Torrdara Forest Walk. Crime might be down but reported breaches of lockdown regulations – real or imagined – were popular enough.

Ian checked the grid reference of the forest walk where the strange man had been seen with the location of Mary Johnson's house, *Cois Dara*. Put that together with the satellite images from Google maps and he could see that the man had been spotted close to the cottage. He had a curious coincidence on his hands, that was all. Ian shook his head and reached for his jacket and car keys. Time to go and interview the neighbours in Torr about the unexplained death.

***

Sid and Edith hadn't spent such an exciting day since lockdown had commenced – and for some considerable time before that. Once the initial shock of their neighbour's unexpected decease had worn off, they enjoyed the activity that event generated. They were very sorry that a woman had died and been so alone that no one had noticed, but they didn't sorrow personally as they had never known her. They were detached from the emotion usually associated with such an ordeal and eagerly watched the ensuing activity from their front window. Sid pushed his favourite recliner closer to the view. With unabashed curiosity he watched the unfolding drama and frequently called Edith to similarly spectate.

Early in the day, a couple of cars had arrived – a marked police car, and an ordinary-looking vehicle which was probably, declared Sid, the forensic, crime scene people. They weren't entirely sure what process a '*suspicious death*' followed, but they could picture people in those white paper suits they had seen on TV, putting out numbered markers, dusting for fingerprints, and whatever else they had to do. They were entranced when more police tape was added; a waving yellow strip was visible through a bush on their boundary.

When an unmarked white van arrived, "Edith! It's the van for the body!" called Sid.

Edith came hurrying back to the window, catching only a glimpse of the van's taillight as the vehicle crunched onto the gravel next door.

Edith was doubtful. "How do you know it's for the body?"

"What else could it be? They wouldn't use a *real* ambulance — there's no need. I've heard they use unmarked vans for bodies — to be discreet. They're hardly going to put up a sign, like they do for babies and such nowadays, '*body on board*'! They don't want people driving down the road imagining the van in front is carrying a *body*!"

Edith's silence spoke consternation and disapproval. She had never imagined what they drove bodies around in — apart from funeral hearses, of course. "I don't think it's right comparing *babies on board* with *bodies on board*," she said at last. "That doesn't sound very nice at all."

Sid huffed in exasperation. *That wasn't his point…*

Edith sighed. "Poor woman." She had already voiced this sentiment several times that morning. "Not even a proper burial!"

"They're not going to bury her yet! Young Ian said they would be taking her to the police mortuary first."

'Young Ian' — DS Ian Prentice — had paid a visit to Sid and Edith that morning, the first of his enquiries in the neighbourhood. Sid wished that there was more they could have told him — any small detail about the woman who had lived mere metres away from them for — "was it a couple of years, Edith?"

"Three," Edith replied. She had checked her diary before Ian's arrival. She told him she always noted "significant dates." It was *definitely* three years.

Ian had looked very smart and official at their doorstep; they were proud they knew him personally. He wore a suit and tie and a mask and stood at least two metres away from where they were on their front step. He nodded politely at everything they said and wrote things down.

"Were you on first name terms with her?"

Edith was eager to corroborate that. "Oh yes, I expect so. She was called Terri, wasn't she?"

Ian looked at the name *Tanya Fletcher* in his notebook. "The house is registered to a Tanya Fletcher," he said. At least, so the police understood from Council Tax and Electoral Roll records.

"I said it wasn't *Terri*," remarked Sid. He was apologetic. "You know what she's like, son, she hears things wrong sometimes."

"When did you last see her?"

They were hopelessly uncertain about that. "We're shielding, you see," Edith said earnestly, as if that explained everything.

"We haven't been out since lockdown began," said Sid. "We can't see her through the hedge, and we don't usually hear anything anyway. She's very quiet. She doesn't even mow her lawn!"

Soberly, Edith added, "We could just *smell* her." Ian was thankful that his smile was literally masked. 'Aunt Edith' wasn't intending to be funny.

With hushed solemnity, Edith added, "I think there was a man there. I'm not drawing any conclusions, mind you, but there might have been *a man*. There was a gruff voice. You could just hear it through the wall."

Sid was surprised. "Are you sure, dear? You never told me."

Edith crossed her arms. "I didn't want to judge."

Sid shook his head. "I don't see why it's *judging* to observe there was a *man*," he remarked. Ian finished scribbling *possible boyfriend?*

on his pad and hastily interrupted another quaint discussion between them to ask if there was anything else they could recall which might help.

After a moment's reflection, Edith offered, "I don't think she had many friends."

Sid observed, "I'm not sure that's what Ian meant by helpful, dear." Regretfully he added, "I think we can only offer you information about the smell. And we've already covered that."

Edith watched as Ian walked away. "*Such* a nice young man! What a shame we can't ask him to stay for tea!"

They re-entered their quiet home and reluctantly left the drama on the other side.

CHAPTER 4

Wednesday 29 April 2020 continued

Walking away from *The Burrow*, the Segrave's modest home, Ian reflected how much you could learn about people from their surroundings. Even without knowing them personally, the neat driveway, trimmed edges, tub of daffodils standing in a pristine pot close to the front door, all spoke of a diligent care, of traditional tastes, of pleasure in simple things.

He was not so sure what to make of their neighbour's dwelling. His first impression of – he glanced at the details on his phone – of *Amanda Finnes'* home was restless, uncoordinated clutter. There were three bright, ceramic butterflies fixed to the pebbledash-rendered wall. A grumpy-looking garden gnome was fishing on an empty birdbath that needed cleaning. Competing artificial and real bushes were in tubs by the front door. There was a small, electric doorbell, but a large, garish brass knocker, more suited to a stately home, had been added to the brown-painted door. Closer inspection revealed it to be *The Green Man* of pagan origin. The door mat had an ancient pentacle symbol on it, identified with magic. He would peg Amanda Finnes with an identity crisis – and possibly deeply insecure.

The opened door revealed an ethereal-looking lady in her fifties with very light-grey eyes. Her mouth was set in a gentle upward curve without really being a smile. All her features were extremely pale – in contrast with her long, dyed-black hair which framed her face symmetrically, and from which she peered, as if through dark curtains.

18

"Yes?" she said.

"Sorry to disturb you … Miss Amanda Finnes?"

"*Ms.*" She spoke softly, almost apologetically, and yet Ian was left with the feeling that he had just committed a great faux pas.

"*Ms* Finnes. I'm sorry to tell you there's been an unexplained death in your neighbourhood and we're canvasing the area for information which might help with our enquiries…"

"*Dead?*" she blurted. She blanched and suddenly clutched the doorframe. Then she appeared to rouse herself and smiled wanly at Ian. "Sorry," she said, "I'm psychic and news of death can affect me. I can feel their passing, you know?"

Ian *didn't* know, but he was intrigued to see where the conversation led. "Did you know her well?"

"Who exactly…?" She was fencing, and yet, aside from her psychic claim, Ian had a feeling there *was* something she knew.

"When did you get the feeling of someone passing?"

Her light eyes suddenly lost their doggy appeal and became suspicious. "I don't recall … *who* are *you* here about? *Who's* died?"

"Unfortunately, your neighbour two doors down, living at a house called … *Cumfrubrum.*" He had to look at his notes to recall the name; *why did people give their homes such peculiar titles?* "Unfortunately, she is deceased, and we are…" He fixed on the curious expression on the woman's face. This was definitely unwelcome, even shocking, news to her. "I'm sorry," he said. "Were you very close to her?"

She was flustered at that question. "No! No, of course not – that is, I didn't really know her at all! Just a neighbour, but – but death is so *shocking?* You know? Especially if you're *sensitive* to the spirit realm. *You* know what I mean?" She took a tentative step closer, peering up into Ian's eyes. "*You* know," she repeated earnestly.

Ian had no illusions she had detected a special spiritual awareness in him. *What was her game? Was she a clever actress trying to conceal something? Or sincere about her beliefs?* "Can you tell me about the person you thought had died?"

Her pale eyes widened. "No, there was no one else, at least there probably is, isn't there? I mean, people die all the time, even somewhere as lovely as this!" She spread her arm in a gesture, once more stepping closer to Ian. "They travel an unknown road which you and I will one day take to them." For one startling moment he thought she meant the two of them would die together. He took a step back to safer distance, glad of the excuse coronavirus gave for space. "Yes, you know too," she murmured. Then she added, "But to think that Tanya has passed on. How did it happen?"

Ian's expressionless tone gave nothing away; nor did his explanation. "We're at the preliminary stages of our enquiries. You obviously knew your neighbour; when did you last see her?"

She was flustered. "Well *no* – not *really* know her. *You* know what it's like, neighbours come and go, and you don't *really* know them. *You* know."

It seemed Amanda Finnes attributed to him not only spiritual awareness, but special understanding. "When did you last see her?" Ian repeated.

Amanda sighed. "*You* know what it's like," she said. "It's been so difficult to keep track – you know, what with the virus and lockdown, every day feels the same."

Apparently she felt Ian knew a great deal. Apart from the information he wanted.

"Did you see her in the last couple of weeks?"

Amanda huffed a deep sigh. "I can't be sure. No, no, I don't think so. I wish now I had, of course, perhaps she was lonely…?"

She was peering closely at him again, fishing for a reaction, hoping to figure out how her neighbour had died. Amanda must know it was statistically unlikely a woman in her forties had died from natural causes. *Was she guessing she might have taken her own life?* "I might have seen her walking along the road, perhaps, in the last month, say. I would have waved, but I hadn't spoken to her for – I don't know – ages, I suppose."

Ian knew when to walk away – at least for now. Amanda was happy to talk about being furloughed off work (she usually worked for a travel firm); she confided in him that she hoped to write a best-selling novel during lockdown; she invited him to join the summer solstice celebration at the ancient stone circle in the strath; she seemed happy to talk about anything *but* her neighbour's death.

Ian moved on to the next neighbour – to a spacious two-storey house which looked like it had been lifted from a modern estate in town and plonked, quite by accident, in the wrong place. Thick fir trees effectively screened the house from all around and made its incongruous appearance a surprise. Cultivated greenery, in fact, nature's influence in general, was kept to an absolute minimum; all around the house it flourished abundantly, but inside the boundary of *The Retreat*, every possible inch was gravelled or slabbed. Neat and bleak.

A dog barked as Ian approached the door and a curtain twitched shortly thereafter. The front door was open when he reached it; Ian stood two metres back and gave his opening spiel.

Mr Robert Geddes, who introduced himself as 'Bob', was wearing a stained T-shirt, baggy joggers and nothing on his feet. He appeared to be a relatively young retiree and confirmed this by explaining to Ian that they had moved to the area a couple of years back, when he sold his car business in London. He seemed more intrigued than concerned at a death close by. "*Who's* dead?" he asked, then without waiting for a response he added, "Caff will want to know about this! She knows some of the folk hereabouts … Caff! CAFF!"

"I heard you the first time!" Cath Geddes, drying her hands on a towel, joined them at the door, standing one step above Bob. She was a tall, slim lady in her fifties or sixties. She was likely a decade older than Amanda Finnes but would certainly beat her neighbour in any test of fitness. She had close-cropped grey hair which was an eye-catching contrast to fine, dark eyes and smooth, tanned skin. Even without the step, she might still be taller than her squat, thick-set husband, and her effortless elegance was a contrast to his overweight slovenliness.

"Police officer," Bob said. "Come about a local death. Where did you say it was?"

Ian hadn't yet. "Three doors down. The house is called *Cumfrubrum*." He remembered this time.

"Never heard of it," Bob said firmly. "D'you know the folk there, Caff?"

Cath was clearly more concerned about Sid and Edith Segrave than with the news that there was a death in the last cottage on the row. "Next door to Sid and Edith? Are they OK?"

"They're fine. Did you know the person who lived in the house adjoining theirs?"

Cath shook her head. "I don't think I ever met her, though I think I've seen her passing. It was a woman, right? What was her name? Maybe that will ring a bell."

"We've yet to formally identify her. According to official records, she was Tanya Fletcher. Does that sound familiar at all?"

Bob was shaking his head. "How'd she die, then? Was she old?"

"We're not sure how she died. We're at the start of our investigation, and there may be nothing untoward. It's police procedure to treat an unexplained death as suspicious until we can prove otherwise."

Cath commented, "I don't think she was old." She sounded faintly puzzled.

"Is there anything else you can tell me? Anything you've seen or heard which is unusual?"

"Nothing *I* can think of. Caff?"

Cath shook her head. "I can't think of anything. Seems a shame we didn't know her, but that's the way it was. We've got plenty of friends around here, but I always got the impression whoever lived there kept herself to herself."

CHAPTER 5

Wednesday 29 April 2020 continued

Amanda watched the plain-clothed detective walk away and sent a frantic WhatsApp message. Then she grabbed her jacket from a peg by the back door and, with a whispered apology to Faroe, quietly left the house. Through a gap in the thick foliage on her boundary, she could glimpse the police officer chatting to Bob and Cath and faintly hear voices. Hopefully they would be there a while; with any luck, Cath wouldn't observe her.

Bordering the field where the three neighbours met, was an ancient, pine forest, named *Hangman's Wood*. It encroached into Cath and Bob's view and was only a short distance away from Amanda's back door. Amanda picked her way through the wood until she was well concealed by the close-packed firs and pines. It was dry underfoot. Very little moisture penetrated the evergreen umbrella which encased the forest; once you were below the treetops, it was perpetually shaded. Only in small patches, green moss and sturdy woodland fauna grasped snatches of filtered light and survived in the shadowed terrain.

Amanda slumped against the base of a thick pine trunk, leaning her head against the rough bark and shutting her eyes.

Tanya was dead!

Terry must have killed Tanya!

Could there be any other explanation?

Was it only the beginning of the year that she had been so happy with Terry? After a messy divorce and subsequent broken relationships, he had seemed the final answer – and the last chance. He didn't say much about himself; with hindsight, she realised how little she knew about him. But men were like that, weren't they? Tall, dark, passably handsome in a rough-and-ready kind of way, he had seemed keen enough on her. While it lasted. Lending him five thousand pounds – the bulk of her meagre savings – had seemed the obvious thing to do at the time; she had ignored the nagging doubts about where he went, how he lived, and what he was doing when he wasn't with her.

How had it come to this?

Around the time she and Terry broke up in February, she met Lisette. Lisette and her other half, Ken, had just moved to rented accommodation in Torr. Lisette was full of advice and comfort; she was exactly the right friend for those hard times. It was she who had first alerted Amanda to Terry's *other* women; through her, Amanda discovered his affair with Tanya Fletcher. Lisette seemed to know so much about Terry that Amanda wondered whether she'd also had an affair with him. *Was it because of Terry that Lisette had moved to the area?*

Amanda always felt a bit like a puppet on a string so far as Lisette was concerned: she must dance to Lisette's tune and so long as everything went Lisette's way all was well. Then, the first time Amanda had used her own initiative – by taking Terry's briefcase of money – their entire friendship had soured. But much as she was ambivalent about Lisette, she was the only person Amanda could turn to now. Everything had changed: *Tanya was dead! Had Terry suspected her of taking the money? Would she – or Lisette – be next?*

Lisette's home was on the other side of the wood from Amanda's. Amanda watched her picking her way through the trees – as usual attired in expensive country brands, looking effortlessly right. That was like Lis: appropriate for every occasion. She was the kind of person you would want at the most awkward family gathering; she seemed to have the uncanny ability to be whatever you most needed in the moment. But the more Amanda had seen of her, the less she felt she knew her. *What was the real Lisette like?*

As soon as she was close enough, Amanda blurted out the news about Tanya, instantly annoyed that Lisette didn't seem particularly surprised, or empathetically panicked either.

"Did you already know about this?" demanded Amanda.

"No, of course not! I didn't really know Tanya of course, but I don't think *Terry* and the money have anything to do with her death. How could they?" She made it sound ludicrous; made Amanda feel stupid.

"Come on!" snapped Amanda. "You know what Terry's like! He must be mixed up in all-sorts to have that much cash in a briefcase! If he thinks Tanya took his money, he probably killed her for it!"

Lisette didn't even attempt to hide her impatience. "You *can't* jump to that conclusion! You said yourself that Terry never mentioned the money to you – in fact, he *borrowed* money from you! I doubt he mentioned his case of banknotes to anyone else, including Tanya!"

Amanda's voice became shrill. "Tanya's *dead*! What kills a healthy woman like her?! *She's younger than me!* It must be that he's found out about the money and thinks it was her!"

Lisette kicked a pinecone across the dry forest floor. "Stop! You'll only give yourself a migraine worrying about it, and then you won't be good for anything!" Lisette sounded anything *but* sympathetic with a potential migraine. "You must keep calm about this! I don't think Tanya's death has got anything to do him! If Terry visits the cottage on *Fridays*, he probably doesn't even know his precious case is missing yet!"

Amanda massaged her forehead, as if a migraine wasn't far away. "That's all very well for you – *you* didn't take the case!"

Lisette forbore to go back over old ground. She admitted – to herself at least – that she had vastly underestimated Amanda: her desire for revenge against Terry; her need to recover the five thousand pounds she was owed; her surprising courage and resourcefulness in snatching a sudden opportunity. Incredibly, it seemed that Amanda had not only been watching Terry's Friday afternoon jaunts to Molly Johnson's cottage far more closely than Lisette realised, but she had actively prepared to intervene. Knowing that Terry's main interest lay in a padlocked shed, Amanda had searched *'How to crack a combination lock'* on YouTube and watched several videos. Perhaps even more surprisingly, it had worked. Finding and removing the silver aluminium briefcase from the shed had, according to Amanda, been spur-of-the-moment. She claimed she had no idea what it contained – in fact, she was pretty sure it *couldn't* be money because it was so heavy. She simply thought that taking it would hurt – or at the very least inconvenience – Terry.

Lisette had come upon Amanda with the briefcase shortly after she had removed it from Terry's hiding place. Amanda was talking to Cath Geddes in the field behind their houses, asking *her* to watch it for a night or two – along with a farfetched explanation why she needed her to do this. Before Lisette could intervene and suggest *she* took the case for safekeeping, the deed was done. Cath, older but toned and muscled through constant workouts, had hoisted at least fifteen kilos of case through her garden gate and whisked it out of sight.

Why didn't you ask me? Lisette had asked the question and Amanda had explained that she *had* intended asking Lis to hide the case, but Terry knew Lis, didn't he? She didn't want to put her friend in any danger. Lisette was definitely *not* convinced by this explanation; ever since, she was *not* the sensitive friend she had been.

Suddenly, Amanda said abruptly, "We should put the case back. It's not worth the risk. You know what he's like! And if you're right and he doesn't know it's missing yet, he'll never know anything about it."

Lisette was staring at the dry forest floor. Slowly her foot moved in a circle, shifting pine needles and dirt with the toe of her Dubarry boots. "Yes, perhaps we should," she conceded. "We can talk to Cath tonight." She wasn't sure how she had become part of the *we* in Amanda's plan which had been so spontaneously and exclusively solo. But it suited her plans to keep Amanda close. *Because of Terry.*

It was, after all, the reason she had befriended her to start with.

***

Cath couldn't remember how their evening meetings in the field behind their houses had started. They became established with the Covid lockdown, perhaps because Amanda and Lisette were now working from home and needed to escape at the end of the day. She had enjoyed the evening chats – until now.

What had she got herself into? She hardly knew these women, and suddenly she felt like she was in the thick of a ridiculously far-fetched mystery. The other two were huddled by Amanda's fence, speaking in hushed tones but seeming friendly enough as she approached. *Could she trust them?*

The story about Molly, about whom Cath knew nothing but that she had lived in a ramshackle cottage nearby and was elderly, was that Molly had asked Amanda to temporarily look after her life savings. This was because she didn't want her only relative, her good-for-nothing nephew, Terry-something, to know anything about her money. Amanda had further convinced Cath that she and Lisette couldn't hide the briefcase themselves as Terry knew they were Molly's friends and, if he suspected it existed, might come looking for it. The arrangement was only for a few days while Terry visited (he was allegedly in a lockdown 'bubble' with Molly), then they could return the case.

Now Molly was dead, and the shock of that unforeseen complication had somewhat worn off. The others were right – she was an old lady well into her eighties; she could quite conceivably die at home without any cause for suspicion. Even the unexpected police presence in the area the previous evening, and the questions earlier that day, didn't seem like such a big deal now. The death of another local woman was coincidence … *wasn't it?*

But if Molly's only next of kin, this nephew Terry, didn't know a case of money even existed, if *they* might be the only people who knew there was such an inheritance waiting to be claimed, why were Amanda and Lisette suddenly so twitchy about returning it? Or would they simply split it between the two of them once Cath had given it up?

What should she do? She could imagine what Bob would say about it all – if he only knew. He wouldn't baulk at it; if Bob knew about the alleged money hidden in their garage, he would contrive a cunning plan to exclude the other two (he would have no compunction how this was achieved) and keep it all.

"I think keeping it might be a crime," said Amanda. She was sipping the odd tea she drank; the others had politely refused her offer of the nettle and cowslip brew.

Cath retorted, "The only *crime* is that the government would tax it all away!" She didn't count irregularities with Her Majesty's Revenue and Customs as wrongdoing.

"I don't mind taking it back to the cottage," said Lisette. She was trying to stop Monty leaping Amanda's fence and reaching small Faroe. "Monty! Here, boy!"

Cath eyed Lisette suspiciously. While lugging the heavy, locked briefcase through the tangle of Hangman's Wood and the remaining distance to Molly's cottage was a thankless task, it *wasn't* if *you kept all the money!* And, judging by the weight of the case, there *must* be a considerable amount inside!

Cath listened and let the others discuss and dictate; she had serious doubts about their explanation of the whole affair; she began to wonder about *them* – about how two such different women came to be friends – and if not friends, *what were they?* Business associates running some kind of illegal scam? Were other hapless residents in the strath caretaking other locked briefcases for them?

Oddly enough, unsuspecting Bob made the decision for that evening. He came into the back garden calling for 'Caff' – "someone on the phone, love," he said. Whatever the reason, Cath was glad to escape. It gave her one more night to decide what to do.

She heard one of them call something about tomorrow night. She waved her hand; she wasn't promising anything.

Yes, they might have taken Molly Johnson's money for safekeeping; but now Molly was dead and the cash was stored in *her garage.*

CHAPTER 6

Thursday 30 April 2020

Cath flicked the switch on the coffee machine and stared blearily through the kitchen window. Outside was frosty; a cold, still morning, and only the birds, and her, were awake. It was 6am, and tired though she was, sleep eluded her. Her mind simply would not rest. *What to do about that money…?* Was it possible she could keep at least some of it? They had spent more than they intended on their 'forever home' in Torr. They had moved there when they sold Bob's used car dealership – his final 'business venture'. Cath wanted a fresh start away from their home, and contacts, in London. She'd always loved the countryside, and she was thinking of Cable, their golden Labrador, too, although not particularly of Bob who hated the country. But he let Cath have her way. Once they'd paid 'back taxes' that Bob had 'forgotten' about, they hadn't enough savings left for the camper van, let alone the world cruise, they had planned. In fact, there wasn't much left for luxuries at all.

Was it possible that Molly had somehow accumulated thousands of pounds in cash in her home? Eccentric people *had* been known to do as much. But banknotes had unique numbers, didn't they? Were they all recorded somewhere? Could you get caught spending it, and charged with theft or something? Cath hadn't even seen inside the case. She only had Lisette and Amanda's word that it contained money – and exactly how much she had no idea. Could she open it, despite the combination lock? Whichever way she looked at it, the story of cash in a case was crazy and possibly criminal. *But it might be true. It might just be lifechanging for their retirement. Should she tell Bob?*

She was no more decided when, fortified with strong coffee in a travel mug, she took Cable out and headed for the local forest walk. Not Hangman's Wood – an impenetrable jungle – but Torrdara Forest Walk, a beauty spot with dirt paths and enough wildness for Cable to scamper and play. No one was about at this still-early hour, except – up ahead she could see a young woman jogging briskly through the twists and turns of the forest, disappearing from sight. Emily Wilson, her other neighbour.

Emily lived in the neat single-storey house, named *Cobwebs*, which bordered Cath on the opposite side to Amanda's home. *Cobwebs* overlooked Hangman's Wood but at its boundary the trees were thinner and allowed glimpses of the scenery beyond, including of the field where the neighbours met.

One evening, early in lockdown, Emily had been working on the border of her garden and Cath had called to her. Emily, accompanied by her friendly border collie, Peter, had climbed her back fence and emerged from the trees to join the other three for a while. For some reason the conversation had stuck fast in Cath's mind.

There was an intriguing mix of worldviews that evening. A remark made by Lisette – who presented her ideas as unquestionable fact – started the discussion. Somehow, they got into the topic of how the world began and whether there was a god or good and evil and such.

Lisette was characteristically categorical. The Big Bang, then the process of evolution, brought everything to its current state. It's been proved as fact for years. What we see around us is all there is. End of story. She was incredulous that anyone could believe the fable of Adam and Eve at the start of the Bible. *Fable* is the way Cath thought of it too.

Emily *actually believed* the Bible's account and questioned Lisette's 'facts'. "But where did the first physical matter come from?" she asked.

Lisette had no answer for the 'creation' of the first material which mysteriously appeared in nothingness, from which the Big Bang had allegedly started the process for an ordered universe[1]. "But you have to answer the same question," she retorted, "only, *you* have to explain who made God!"

Emily's responded, "But I'm not claiming that God is material at all or made of physical matter the way the world is. The Bible says that God is spirit. He's not something that *can* be created. But that's not true of the universe."

Interestingly, Amanda, despite admiring elements of the Bible, firmly disagreed with the creation tale as well. "It's just a fable with life-lessons, like lots of the Bible. As if it could be true that God would make a perfect world, then punish a young couple with banishment and death for their first tiny mistake! It's like an artist seeing part of their picture ruined but refusing to simply repaint a bit and put it right again. If this story was true, God would have forgiven mistakes and given people another chance!"

Cath didn't think that there could be any reasonable rejoinder to this, but Emily explained, "I think of the picture analogy differently. Imagine a beautiful painting of a perfect world, created by a loving, all-powerful God. In it, He placed two people – who were made to be like Him, meant to represent His interests on earth – His caretakers, as it were, acting like Him, carrying out His

---

[1] Where the first physical matter came from is still a mystery and remains unanswered by scientists.

wishes, responsible for guarding and keeping everything He had made. Because they were perfect, they understood God's instructions precisely, and He told them that there was one thing they could not do. It would test their love for Him. Would they trust that He knew best for them with this one command not to eat of the tree which gave knowledge not only of good, but of evil?"

It was a surreal moment, listening to her describe the world like that, however unlikely it was to be true.

Emily continued. "So, they could do things God's way – in His own creation which was designed to fit His rules – or they could decide that they knew better than their Creator. They were offered another way – eat the fruit God told you not to eat, and you'll be able to decide your own good and evil. You won't be bound by God's restrictions, you can make up your own rules, which can change according to the way you want the world to be. And so they made their choice, and their decision to dictate their own rules and run the world on their own terms, is pretty much the mindset today.

"But to return to the painting analogy: it wasn't simply that they spoiled part of the picture, but they moved into another painting entirely, of which *they* wanted to be the artists! They thumbed their noses at the Great Artist of the Universe and basically said they'd rather paint the world around them themselves, thank you very much, not the way their Originator depicted it. And so it has been, all the years since … people writing their own rules, deciding their own version of truth…"

And so it was. Here Cath was, a few weeks later, facing a quandary about some alleged money, writing her own rules as if there was no definite right or wrong about it. *And there wasn't, was there…?* Cath knew what Emily, now long vanished out of sight, would say. She would say God decreed what was right and wrong. But Cath wasn't sure He existed, and if He did, He had never shown any interest in anything she did.

She returned to the house no more decided what to do about the money than when she'd left it.

But she never got to decide.

When she opened the back door, Bob was waiting for her.

Cable ran eagerly to Bob and pushed his nose into his hand, begging for a treat. Bob touched the dog's head absentmindedly, his eyes never leaving Cath. "When were you going to tell me?"

In the first few seconds, Cath didn't twig why Bob was blocking her route from the back door into the kitchen, arms crossed, eyes glaring, geared up for a fight. "Tell you what?"

Bob unfolded his arms and began to slap a bound wad of ... Suddenly, she froze. "You...?" Incredulity nipped her voice into shrill indignation. "You found...?"

"Yeah, I found the money, the whole *fortune*. So, I repeat. When. Were. You. Going. To. Tell. ME?"

There was only one way to meet Bob when he was enraged – and that was with equal rage. Their years together had withstood many such storms. All the frustration, the uncertainty, the tiredness, the confusion – all spilled into a fierce explosion of fury that battered Bob. He didn't shrink under the onslaught; he gave as good as he got. When the shouting died down, when they had exhausted every accusation they could think to hurl at each other, when the details emerged through their convoluted, constantly digressing arguments, they settled once more into the default mould which had lasted their turbulent marriage. At bottom, Bob believed that Cath would have told him about the cash at some point and not run off to spend it on her own; at bottom, Cath believed that Bob could help her solve the dilemma in which she found herself. Bob further proved his support by frying sausages and eggs, making an impromptu cooked breakfast – it was still only 7.30am – while Cath sat with her feet up, cradling another strong coffee and warming her hands.

"They mustn't find out that you know about the money. They said not to tell anyone else."

Bob agreed. "Yes, let them think it's only you they're dealing with. Play along acting dumb for now."

Cath nodded.

Bob flipped a sausage over in the pan. "We can't be too careful."

Cath eyed Bob dubiously over her coffee mug. "I don't want any trouble." Back in the day, Bob – who described himself by the vague term *in business* – had made his money, plenty to keep them comfy in their retirement and buy the house Cath wanted. Cath had never asked too many questions and frankly never cared about his shadier dealings. His way of being *in business* had occasional interesting repercussions; he still knew people who, for a sum, could make problems go away… "The last thing we want is the police checking into your past," she added. If Bob wasn't concerned about others, he might at least act in his own interests.

Bob began to serve up. "Nothing to worry yourself about, sweetheart." He placed her full plate on a tray and brought it across to her. He poured himself a coffee and picked up his own tray. For once, the telly was off. There were more important things to discuss.

They had one million pounds in their garage!

One million pounds!

CHAPTER 7

Cath still couldn't believe it. Not even when Bob showed her the bundles of banknotes he had carefully removed from the forcibly opened, now slightly bent and buckled case. Each note was a Bank of Scotland banknote worth one hundred pounds sterling (at least the notes on the outside of the stacks were). So far as Bob could estimate, there were one thousand notes in each bundle – secured with an official-looking thick paper strip. Each bundle was subdivided ten straps of around one hundred notes each. That was a grand total of one hundred thousand pounds in each wad! There were ten stacks in two rows of five. That meant … one million pounds! It was a staggering, unbelievable, *life-changing* discovery.

Although some of the bundles appeared as if they'd been tampered with, Bob didn't undo them. He handled them with the blue disposable gloves they'd stocked up on thanks to Covid. He was every bit as incredulous as Cath had been that an old lady had such a stash of cash. *How? Why? Was it traceable? Were the notes legitimate?* Furthermore, the briefcase was one of those official-looking aluminium ones, with black eggbox foam in the lid. It looked borrowed from a movie set, "Like those films where big payoffs are made. They use cases like this!" said Bob. *How had Molly Johnson obtained such a thing?*

Bob wasn't one to worry overmuch about *how* such things had come about. He had a practical mind, and the first order of business was to determine the banknotes' authenticity. Lockdown complicated things – they couldn't simply go into a bank with a one-hundred-pound note and ask to have it checked; supermarkets were open but, to avoid the spread of Covid, they were encouraging payment by card, not cash; they certainly couldn't spend it at the local shop where Elspeth would undoubtedly show it to everyone who came in; in addition, she likely wouldn't have a clue whether it was legitimate or not until it vanished into whatever banking system she was linked with. They might never know if it was real through that source.

"Look it up on the computer, Caff," said Bob.

"I don't see how that will help!" Cath was irritable, still feeling the effects of a sleepless night. And now that she knew for sure how much money she was 'looking after' she wasn't *less* worried; with that amount and Bob involved she was even more anxious.

"Well, you won't know it'll help if you don't try, will you?" retorted Bob. "Use the google-thingy and ask it how you know if banknotes are real."

Cath didn't suppose 'google-thingy' would be much help, but, grumbling, she turned on the laptop. She knew exactly how to use Google, but she wasn't inclined to be quickly cooperative with Bob's commands. She took her time finding the Google icon, then slowly typed '*how do you know banknotes are real*' into the space intended for the enquiry. Then she hit the return key. The computer didn't pause for long before numerous results flooded the screen.

"What's it say?" asked Bob.

"There are over sixteen million results! It says so at the top of the page!"

Bob ran his fingers through his thinning hair. "Never mind about that, what does the first one say?"

"It says, '*Run your finger across the paper note and if it's genuine, you'll be able to feel raised print on areas such as the words 'Bank of England' on the note…*'"

"This is Bank of *Scotland*, Caff!"

"Well, they're hardly going to be different, are they?" snapped Cath.

"How do you know they're not?"

Cath ignored his question and continued reading. "*If it's a counterfeit note, it's likely to have a textured feel to it and will feel flat all over* … That doesn't make sense!"

"I can hear *that*," grumbled Bob.

"There's another one here, it's about *colour-shifting ink*, and you look for the *portrait watermark of President Jackson…*"

"That's American dollars you're on now! Caff!"

"Well, I don't know! Just do the first thing it said! Can you feel raised print on the words?"

Slowly, Bob felt the one banknote he had carefully extracted from a bundle. "I might be able to if I wasn't wearing these gloves," he said. "See if there's a picture of a one-hundred-quid Scottish note."

"I don't know how to find pictures!" Cath typed '*what does a £100 Scottish banknote look like?*' into the box. She hit the return key and was pleasantly surprised when an image was offered to her without her figuring out how to search for pictures. "There's – well, it's a man in a wig on one side, and…"

"Balmoral Castle on the other!" finished Bob. "These look the same as that, Caff!" He waved a banknote around in his gloved hand.

"Well, I suppose they'd still look like that even if they were fake!"

That was all they could do to ascertain the legitimacy of their treasure. They would have to think of another plan to know for sure. As Bob pointed out, it wasn't as if they had ever seen a one-hundred Scottish banknote before; how would any *normal* person know if it was real? All the same, they were glad it wasn't smaller denomination notes that filled the case.

After a further heated discussion, they hid the case on an untidy shelf in the garage, well-concealed under and behind leftover paint in a dozen tins, a box of spare tiles, and a couple of rolled rugs they didn't need. As Bob pointed out, the upside to lockdown was that no one would be visiting; crime had practically disappeared; the police were never out here.

"Don't meet those women tonight," said Bob, "and don't answer the door if they come calling. They got us into this, they can wait our time now. I'm going to keep an eye on this lady, Molly's, cottage – just to see what's what. Don't you worry about a thing. We'll figure out what to do.

CHAPTER 8

Friday 1 May 2020

Tanya Fletcher's unexpected death didn't appear suspicious after all. Ian had completed door-to-door interviews with close neighbours; there weren't so many to conduct in tiny Torr, so Ian had handled them himself. Nothing of concern was uncovered. It was odd so young a woman should die unnoticed – but not impossible. There were no signs of any *significant other* in Tanya Fletcher's life; her marital status was 'divorced'.

The scene at Ms Fletcher's home, *Cumfrubrum*, had been processed – photographed, dusted for fingerprints and thoroughly tagged and bagged. The matter had been reported to the Procurator Fiscal – the qualified lawyer appointed to investigate unexplained deaths. The autopsy result might take more time than usual given additional precautions because of Covid.

There was nothing new reported on the separate matter of the NCA case of missing money.

***

Bob's instruction not to worry had the opposite effect on Cath. When had Bob's involvement in *anything* ever simplified matters? When had it not led to complications and, occasionally, disaster? After another restless night, Cath soaked in a hot bath, shutting out the world, even as her thoughts continued to run unchecked.

What added to her angst was that she wasn't sure *why* she worried. The money was safely in *her* garage; only two other people, besides her and Bob, knew it was there. But her anxiety was more fundamental than that. It was a nagging concern that it *wasn't right*, and now that Bob was involved there would likely be plenty else that wasn't right about it. What if Bob wanted to exclude the others altogether? Was that fair? Was it wrong to keep money that had belonged to someone else?

Cath was pleased to think that if Molly had still been alive, she would have returned the case; that would only have been right, wouldn't it? Molly might still have needed funds for, say, her care. But since Molly was dead, they weren't defrauding her; *she* didn't need it anymore. By all accounts, Molly hadn't liked her nephew, Terry, and had intended to exclude him from her will. Perhaps he bullied and used her. Cath could just imagine the type and she had no compunction about following Molly's imagined wishes in this matter: there was no way Terry should get the money; it seemed to her that he had less claim on it than she and Amanda and Lisette.

Was she right to act judge and jury in this matter? Was there any real right or wrong about it, or was their only concern that they mustn't get caught?

Cath had googled (at a speed which would have surprised Bob) what Richard Dawkins had to say about the matter. She was comforted that such a clever man had proved there was no God; she was sure he had all the answers to the hard questions about right and wrong and such. She read, *"The universe we observe has precisely the properties we should expect if there is, at bottom, no design, no purpose, no evil and no good, nothing but blind pitiless indifference."*[2]

If that was the case, whatever she did made absolutely no difference. In fact, there was no one to even dictate what was right

---

[2] Richard Dawkins, The Blind Watchmaker: Why the Evidence of Evolution Reveals a Universe Without Design (Norton, New York, 1986)

and wrong. There was the government, of course, and the laws they passed, but neither she nor Bob had ever had much respect for *that* authority. There was no one to judge or condemn; their only consideration was feathering their own nest, and not getting caught in the process.

She thought again of the picture that Emily had described. A Creator. One who had written the rules – who had decreed what was good and what was evil and who had, according to Emily, designed them with a conscience so that they would know what was right and wrong too. Of course, she didn't, *couldn't*, believe *that*. Only one bit was true – that, like Adam and Eve in the Bible story, she and Bob were making up their own rules to suit themselves. And that only, ultimately, mattered if there *really was* God.

While Cath soaked in a bath, Bob took Cable for a walk – an unusual enough occurrence since Cable was really Cath's dog. But Bob felt Cable might serve a useful purpose in his reconnaissance this morning.

Molly's cottage, *Cois Dara* – which was Gaelic for *near the oak tree* – was almost entirely immersed in Torrdara Forest. Once upon a time there must have been at least one oak tree in the wood which lent its name to Molly's old cottage. It was secluded at the end of an overgrown driveway and shrouded by trees and shrubs, completely excluded from the world around, and yet not far from its nearest neighbour. In fact, it was a short walk from Lisette's house and about twenty other houses that formed the bulk of Torr.

Cable did prove useful. Bob found the overgrown entrance to the cottage easily enough. There was only one ramshackle old place that fitted the description and there was a faded wooden sign, on which you could faintly see the *Cois Dara* lettering. Having learnt from Cath that "the name has 'Dara' in it, the same as the forest does", Bob threw the dog's ball part way up the driveway. Cable obligingly sprang after it and Bob began to investigate. He rounded a bend in the potted track and came suddenly upon the white-washed cottage. There were several outbuildings in varying states of decay; out of one a man suddenly emerged.

Bob, seldom at a loss, raised his hand in a bold and friendly gesture. "Alright, mate? Sorry about this, I was just trying to find my dog!"

The man was in his forties, thickset and towered several inches in height above Bob. And if it took a rogue to know one – well, Bob knew one when he saw one. In another setting they might have been 'business associates', but it was abundantly clear from the man's demeanour Bob was *not* welcome here.

He swore at Bob; in return, Bob smiled glibly. "Sorry, mate," he said again. He called Cable and retraced his steps. Bob would've staked his life on the fact that whatever was going on at that cottage was dodgy and *must* be connected with the hoard of cash in his garage. Probably the man was the 'Terry' referred to in the women's story as Molly's nephew. Whoever Terry was, Bob had no doubt that he was a dangerous man to cross.

But he and Cath hadn't crossed him, had they?

If anyone had, it was those women.

CHAPTER 9

That evening, Cath met the women as usual. After Bob's description of the man at Molly's cottage, Cath was even more certain that Amanda and Lisette hadn't told her the truth about the money. Perhaps the man not only *knew* about the funds but was actively *searching* for them. Well, if her neighbours thought that everything was going their way and that she was simply going to hand over the cash, they were badly mistaken.

"We wondered what had happened to you," Lisette said warmly. She seemed relieved to see Cath.

"Where were you last night?" Amanda asked abruptly. Cath's eyes narrowed. Had she been mistaken to think Amanda harmless? Someone who was feeble-minded, and wavering, with stupid mixed-up ideas, but innocuous enough? "I mean, we *missed* you. We thought you might have caught the virus!" Amanda added in her more usual timid tone.

"Oh really? I thought you might have been more worried about the money than me," Cath chuckled, and, while they laughed in response, it was funny to watch their wholly unamused expressions.

Amanda held up a mug in a friendly gesture. "I made us all a drink," she said. Lisette was already holding one. Amanda handed the mug to Cath. "Dandelion and hawthorn," she explained. "It's good for relaxing."

Was it poisoned? Cath mentally shook herself. *How had she moved, in a couple of days, from friendly chats with neighbours to seriously thinking one of them might try to poison her?*

Of course, the answer was in her garage: *one million pounds.*

Anyway, Cath had no intention of sampling the drink. English breakfast tea was good enough for her; Amanda's penchant for herb-type stuff was not something she admired. As the others carried on small talk, filling time before they could tackle her about the money, Cath surreptitiously bent down as if to tie the lace on her trainers. She poured a good quantity of the disgusting tea-brew onto the fresh green grass. She wouldn't have been surprised if the grass had shrivelled on the spot. Amanda had talked about her interest in magic as part of her all-embracive faith, her *'found truth'* as she called it. It seemed to Cath that Amanda put together all the things that she *wished* were true, called them *truth*, and, by some dubious process, thought that made them *true*; but witches and the like didn't *really* have spiritual powers, *did they?* For a moment, Cath even thought about crossing herself.

"We've been thinking how to return Molly's money," said Lisette.

"Oh?" Cath swatted at a fly, as if shifting a million quid about the countryside was of no more significance than that pesky insect. She wondered what they would say about the bent and broken case with several messy drill-holes and the combination lock now permanently out of commission, thanks to Bob.

"We think we should return it to the cottage. As soon as possible."

Cath swatted another fly. *What did they know?* Likely they knew that that chap Terry – or whoever it was Bob had seen – was staking out the place, looking for the cash.

Carelessly, Cath asked, "How will you get in?"

"In?"

"Into the cottage. Now that Molly's dead, I expect it's locked up, isn't it?" Cath couldn't read what Lisette was thinking but nothing seemed to dent her confidence for long. On the other hand, Amanda was hiding behind the big, black sunglasses she sometimes wore when she had a migraine. Judging from the angle of her head, she wasn't looking at either of them. Was she even paler than usual? Worried? *Frightened?*

Lisette commented, "There are outbuildings. We could leave it there."

Amanda chimed in, "We need to give it back." Cath wondered whether she'd been drinking. Perhaps the dark glasses were to compensate for a hangover. Or perhaps her wretched herbal brew accounted for it.

"I could put it back in an outbuilding for you," Cath said blithely. She was amused at the chagrin she saw in Lisette's eyes.

"As long as you do it soon." That was all Amanda seemed concerned about. She was definitely worried about something.

Lisette was decisive. "I'll do it. I can replace it exactly where it was found. That way no one will know it was missing at all."

Cath wondered about mentioning the man who had been at the house earlier in the day. It might have been interesting to see their reaction. Instead, she said, "I thought you said Molly had it in the *house*." She was matter of fact about it, watching them squirm as they tried to recall exactly what they'd told her about where they had collected it from. She couldn't precisely remember herself; but she wasn't going to admit that. *Whatever they were telling her, it wasn't the truth.*

When Cath made no moves to go and retrieve the case as Lisette clearly hoped, "We could give it another day before we decide," Lisette said, as if it didn't matter one way or the other. "Are you happy to hold onto the case a bit longer?"

As if offering a great concession, Cath said, "I suppose that's OK."

Lisette whistled piercingly for Monty, her large dog with posh breeding – which included lots of names like 'labradoodle'. As usual, Monty completely ignored her. Whatever his fine breeding, he enjoyed tasty morsels of dubious origin as much as the next dog. Lisette hauled him off whatever animal droppings he'd been consuming; Cable went obediently to Cath; Amanda rose and at last removed her sunglasses. She vanished through her patio doors, with Faroe waddling behind.

CHAPTER 10

Saturday 2 May 2020

While Cath was out walking Cable on Saturday evening (she decided that not meeting the women every night would keep them on their toes), Bob enacted his own plan. He could only think of one other way of determining whether the extraordinary stash of cash in their garage consisted of real banknotes. Secondary to that was the problem of whether they were stolen, but they would figure that out later. First, they must discover if the notes were authentic – and consequently what risks they should be prepared to take. After all, if they couldn't spend it, they may as well dump it back in the sheds at the old cottage and be done with it.

Ostensibly, he was going to do their weekly shopping. Cath was always delighted when Bob made the slightest effort to help with household chores. She wouldn't suspect a thing until he had the answers they needed.

When he reached the nearest supermarket, ten miles away in Aberlochee, he stood patiently in the queue, two metres back from the person in front. He chose a trolley when he reached the front of the line. At the obligatory cleaning station, he sprayed the trolley with disinfectant and wiped it with a paper towel. He didn't think that was necessary, but he wasn't going to draw attention to himself by breaking the rules. He followed the one-way arrows around the supermarket, filling the cart with most of the things on Cath's list. Early in the proceedings, he bumped into Elspeth from the local shop. The remaining aisles were spent pretending he couldn't see her. He hummed loudly as if completely distracted and once he raced the wrong way down an aisle – as a consequence of which he missed a few items on Cath's list.

He paid with his contactless card and pushed the trolley outside. A quick scan told him that the queue at the banking hole-in-the-wall a short distance away had cleared. Keeping the full trolley with him, he placed it at an awkward angle. Even if someone was inclined to break the two-metre social distancing rule, they couldn't get close. He inserted his card into the slot and chose '*make a deposit*'. He should have put his glasses on, but he thought he managed to input £100.00 for the deposit amount. He tried to appear casual and hummed loudly again, drumming his fingers on the console as if he did this every day – not, like, *never*. An envelope suddenly emerged from a slot, startling him. *Now what?* Fumbling, he removed the one-hundred-pound banknote from his pocket and crammed it in the envelope. He hastily stuck it shut – all wonky but it would have to do. He fed it back into the slot, hoping the creases he'd caused wouldn't jam it. It vanished from view.

***

Even on his day off, Strathavie played in Ian's mind. He spent his free time walking the hills above the strath, enjoying his elevated view of the tiny, scattered houses in the peaceful glen. Sunshine glinted on the river and, closer by, on the untroubled surface of Loch Avie. That anything seriously nefarious could be taking place in that rural idyl seemed ludicrous.

Returning to his car by Loch Avie, he drove back towards the main route through the strath. He hesitated at the junction, then turned right and snaked through the tree-lined road farther down the strath into tiny Inveravie. He turned left between stone pillars standing guard at the entrance to Strathavie House.

It wasn't his first visit to Colonel Urquhart, the local *Laird of the Glen*. He had been to the stone mansion as a schoolfriend of the Colonel's son, Jack – a close friendship which lasted into the present. Jack was absent, but he did have a reason to talk to the Colonel and it was as well done in person as over the phone.

Aside from quizzing Elspeth at the local shop – where everything he asked would become public knowledge – the Colonel was the best source of local knowledge that Ian knew. And the soul of discretion. The Urquhart family had owned vast tracts of land in the area for several hundred years, including their substantial home at Strathavie House. Things were not, now, quite as they were in the past – when the local Laird owned lock, stock and barrel everything within his wide reach; things were, at least ostensibly, more *equal* nowadays. But, while plenty of the vast estate had been sold or leased and many houses in the strath were now privately owned, the reach of the Urquharts was not insubstantial. How much land and how many cottages in the area they still owned, no one, not even Elspeth, could guess.

Colonel Urquhart was hurtling down the track in his unpretentious old Land Rover as Ian approached in his car. The Colonel immediately pulled the Land Rover onto the rough verge, and he and Ian stood together in the dappled sunlight under the gigantic trees which screened Strathavie House and farm buildings.

Ian was welcomed warmly. The Colonel not only knew him personally from his friendship with his son, but he also respected Ian's reputation.

"I don't know the name Tanya Fletcher, but I heard Molly Johnson was dead, of course," the Colonel said when Ian had explained the backstory. "Ah," he nodded at the question in Ian's eyes. "You wouldn't necessarily know, but *Cois Dara*, Molly's cottage, belongs to the estate." In other words, to *him*. "It's in a poor state. We've offered improvements over the years, but poor Molly refused interference of any kind. She just wanted to be left in peace. Rather an eccentric and secretive old lady. Her husband was a good forestry worker, but Molly must have outlived him, and been on her own for – well, it must be over twenty years now."

Ian asked, "Who's Mrs Johnson's next of kin?"

The Colonel thought for a moment. "A Mrs Alice Piper, I think is the name we have. A niece, I believe. Her last address was Australia and we're having difficulty contacting her, but we'll be securing the property and taking legal possession in a couple of months. As far as the official paperwork goes, it's only Alice that inherits. Molly may have had other more distant relatives – in fact…" The Colonel paused and then faintly smiled. "I recollect that Terry Vass had some connection with Molly or her late husband. It's possible there's a distant relationship there. Which might explain why Terry has apparently been in and out of the strath – even during lockdown."

Ian inclined his head. "We've long suspected Vass of wider links to organised crime – but he's only ever been lifted for minor offences." The name *Terry Vass* had been among the first on Ian's mental list in connection with NCA case. "I don't suppose you've heard any local rumours about a large sum of cash in the area?"

The Colonel scratched his head, dislodging his tweed cap and then pulling it firmly straight again. "Nothing that I recall. Although, if it's anything to do with Terry Vass, Molly Johnson's cottage would have made a good hiding place! It's so well hidden, and, while she was alive, she resented visitors – so you wouldn't likely be disturbed there."

For the first time since the NCA case had crossed his desk, Ian felt vaguely hopeful. "If you don't mind, Colonel, I'd like to take a look at that cottage."

Since the Colonel had been intending a visit to the cottage to ensure it was secure, he picked up the keys from the estate office and then joined Ian who was already parked at *Cois Dara*. To say that the place was neglected was an understatement. While the Colonel unlocked the door, Ian walked around the perimeter of the property. It was deceptively spacious and contained jumbled outbuildings added at various times, with lean-tos stuck higgledy-piggledy onto just about any available wall. Wood and other materials were stored haphazardly under the makeshift shelters and all over the yard.

"Iain Johnson liked his projects," the Colonel commented drily.

"But it *would* make a pretty good hiding place." Ian looked at a timber workshop that, of all the ramshackle buildings, appeared to have been used more recently. There was a shiny metal flap and hook which could have been secured with a padlock – although there was no sign of it now.

"Definitely put there since Molly was able to do anything," said the Colonel.

The workshop yielded no clues, but a sixth sense made Ian turn suddenly. A man had approached from Torrdara Forest Walk and was watching them through the trees. He was far off the path and turned swiftly away when he was spotted, but on Ian's shout he turned back and grinned sheepishly, waving a ball in his hand.

"Sorry to disturb you, mate, just finding my dog's ball!"

It was Bob Geddes.

CHAPTER 11

Sunday 3 May 2020

Bob had been snooping around like a dog on a scent. He was determined to find a way to keep their unexpected treasure trove. He was blasé about seeing that police detective and Colonel Urquhart at the cottage yesterday.

"There's nothing to connect us, love," he told Cath.

To Cath, it was a familiar path: Bob getting entangled with goodness-knows-what, which he might, if he were lucky, escape from by the skin of his teeth, or land them in … *what?*

Early Sunday morning, over her first blissful cup of strong coffee, Cath distracted herself by googling timeshares in exotic places, and imagining the money – or at least a third of it – was theirs without any further complications. But her dreams were shattered before she'd finished her coffee when Bob, still in his dressing gown, spied *them* from the upstairs window. While he scrambled for his clothes, he shouted urgent instructions to Cath. Which found her grabbing her jacket, throwing a treat to Cable to keep him happy, and slipping into a bitterly cold, still-frosty morning.

The birds were singing despite the frost that thickly coated the outside world. The sun was shining, dancing on the ice crystals, turning frozen moisture into fine diamonds. Cath went briskly through the garden. The catch on the gate into the field was frosted shut; she wished she had worn her gloves.

The tall, crowded trees of Hangman's Wood excluded the frost. Once she was in the forest, the glittering white disappeared but the cold remained. She had never been in the wood before. There was hardly space to move which did not involve being impaled on sharp twigs and branches. Moving as quietly as she could, she began to crawl through the undergrowth, following two familiar voices. She didn't have far to go. She found a fallen tree within earshot and lay flat on the dry dirt ground, refusing to think about wild animals and insects, focussing exclusively on Lisette's and Amanda's hushed tones.

She'd heard it said that listeners never overheard any good of themselves; now she discovered it was true. All her misgivings about how they were using her were right after all; in fact, were worse than she had imagined.

What had she ever done to them? Most of her life she had lived with Bob's double-dealings and despised *his* standards; but she'd lived a fairly good life herself. *And look where it's got me! Doing a favour for neighbours has led to this!*

Amanda's shrill tones were clearly distinguishable. "It doesn't matter if the police haven't found anything yet, I still think Terry killed Tanya! He must have thought *she* took the money!"

The woman who died. The one the police had asked about. They not only think that she was murdered, they think it's in connection with the cash! They know that the money's dangerous.

Lisette was half-heartedly disagreeing with Amanda's assessment. They couldn't know for sure, but yes, she agreed they should definitely put the case back at Molly's.

Cath smiled grimly. *It would serve them right if Terry — whoever he really was — hunted them down for taking it!*

Amanda was concerned that she, Cath, was going to prove difficult. "What if she says she's not giving it back? Or that she's going to put it back and doesn't? What if she decides to keep it? We should never have told her there was money in the case!"

Lisette interjected, "It wasn't *my* idea to give the case to Cath in the first place!" But Amanda wasn't listening.

"I know her type. On the surface she's nice and respectable, but underneath she's greedy and conniving and – and simply doesn't care about the consequences for us! Oh yes, she's the type to land others in it and walk all over our dead bodies!" she said viciously.

"What a shame you didn't know Cath *before* you gave her the case, then!" Lisette snapped.

"She didn't turn up last night, *again*!" Amanda seethed.

Lisette sighed. "If she's not there tonight, we'll knock on the door and ask for it back. If you ask me, she's scared of her husband. She doesn't want him to know about it, but if she knows Terry is dangerous, she'll give it back! Or we'll tell her husband and hopefully *he'll* see sense!"

Well, weren't they in for a nasty surprise?

Cath reported back to Bob, sparing no details. She was bitterly angry at how they had used her; how they had been prepared to land *her* in danger with this man, Terry. She enjoyed Bob's extreme ideas of revenge: knowing most of them to be completely impracticable. Then she took a long bath, hoping to thaw out her cold, stiff body and expunge the grime of the forest.

Since they planned to barricade themselves in their home for the afternoon and evening, she took Cable out for an early walk. Now that the frost had melted, it was a beautiful spring day. Cable was delighted with the outing; Cath hardly noticed her surroundings. She would never admit it to a soul, but she was hurt by her neighbours' betrayal; she was anxious about the money; she wanted plenty of it herself – and now had no compunction about double-crossing her neighbours. So far as she was concerned, there was no one left with any better claim to the money than herself. But the same nagging questions kept playing in her mind: *was there any right or wrong about it? Or was it simply a matter of her and Bob acting in their own interests?*

She wasn't any more inclined to think about God existing, or to worry that He had rules she was breaking and was waiting in vengeful fury to punish her. Science had disproved God (although she didn't know the details). But, for a moment, she imagined what it would feel like if there *was* God. Not about the rule-breaking, punishment bit – she didn't know how she'd ever get around *that* – but what if there was a God who had created her with a purpose? Who not only knew about her, but who cared about the fact that she existed, who cared what happened to her? Who had a plan for her even *after* this life?

She reached the end of the path and began walking the final stretch along the narrow road towards home. *What foolish fancies to imagine life was anything but a sometimes-tragic accident!* There was nothing to do but take advantage of whatever life threw at them and survive as the fittest (and surely one million pounds went a long way to ensure *that!*), before it all ended in *nothing*.

She asked Bob what he thought when she reached home. She knew his answer, but it was good to have her own feelings confirmed.

"*God?*" Bob echoed incredulously. "What's *He* got to do with this?"

Cath asked, "Do you ever think about God and if He's bothered about the things we do?"

"No, I don't! Realised years ago He couldn't possibly be real, else He'd have done something to show us He's there. And if He cared what we did and wanted to judge us, He'd have stopped us long before now, wouldn't He?"

Cath didn't know. When Lisette had joked that if God existed then He should at least show Himself, Emily had said that He had. She claimed that God hadn't stayed away from the problems on earth – that He had come to earth as Jesus Christ. But Jesus had died, hadn't He? So how did that help?

The doorbell rang twice that Sunday night. Bob, spying from the window, saw Amanda walk away from the door towards Lisette who waited at the gate.

He turned the telly up.

Neither he nor Cath answered the door.

When they spotted the scribbled note which had been pushed through their letterbox, Bob read it out loud with relish. '*Ask Cath about the money*' it said. Bob roared with laughter.

CHAPTER 12

Monday 4 May 2020

While he awaited the autopsy result on Tanya Fletcher, Ian was surprised to discover that the fingerprints taken from Ms Fletcher's house matched those of Terry Vass which, since he had been fingerprinted in the last couple of years, were held on the police IDENT1 database. *Did this mean that Tanya's death was suspicious?* There was a connection between Molly Johnson's cottage and Terry Vass; there could well be a connection between Terry Vass and the missing money. *What about Bob Geddes?* That glimpse he had of Bob Geddes on Saturday, peering through the foliage of Torrdara Forest, certainly doing more than looking for his dog's ball, must have meant *something*. Was he also connected with events? Could there be collusion between Terry Vass and Bob Geddes?

Ian typed Robert Geddes' name into the Police National Computer to check for any criminal record. The results certainly made interesting reading.

***

Amanda had another herbal tea concoction ready for Cath, but when she didn't appear again that evening, she and Lisette retreated to Hangman's Wood to decide what to do.

Except, what *could* they possibly do if Cath wouldn't hand back the money? *Report it to the police?* But even if they concocted a good story, if the police believed Cath's version, they could be implicated in anything from theft or receiving stolen goods – to being part of whatever Terry was involved in. And that might include Tanya's *murder*.

Well, at least Terry wouldn't think to look for the money at the Geddeses'; he couldn't possibly know that the funds were concealed by a local couple with whom he had no connection. As a disguise, it was effective. But now the cash was completely out of reach.

Amanda maintained, "If Cath doesn't give the money back tonight, I think we should call the police. I know," she held up her hand at Lisette's protest, "I know we might be implicated. But not if we report it *anonymously*. The officer who called left a card with an anonymous reporting number on it."

Lisette smirked. Amanda enjoyed referring to the good-looking detective who had called about Tanya's death. Aloud, she said, "Whatever we do, I agree there's no way Cath and – what's her husband's name again? – right, *Bob*. There's no way they can keep the money! Let's wait and see if Cath turns up with it tonight."

With some relish, Amanda said, "I wonder if Bob killed Cath after he found our note and discovered the money."

Lisette watched through narrowed eyes as Amanda traipsed back to her house through the scant trail in the dim wood. There was a detached callousness about Amanda which was quite unnerving – more so because it was hidden beneath her fragile, sensitive demeanour. How desperate was she to get the money back? Would she do something stupid – *again*?

Whatever she seemed to be, Amanda had already proved she could be surprisingly bold and resourceful. She had already extracted a million quid from under the nose of a criminal such as Terry Vass, *and* successfully secreted it at her neighbour's; what might she do next?

Was she really what she seemed?

CHAPTER 13

Tuesday 5 May 2020

When Cath didn't appear on Tuesday evening, Amanda had had enough. If Cath thought she could keep the money, with all the repercussions that this might have for her and Lisette with Terry (she didn't count Cath's ignorance in this matter any excuse), well, Cath could think again. Amanda picked up the card by her phone. As well as DS Ian Prentice's contact details, it contained the anonymous freephone Crimestoppers number.

She made the call and hoped the police would do the rest.

She didn't plan to tell Lisette.

CHAPTER 14

Wednesday 6 May 2020

It had been a few days since Bob had deposited the banknote in his account. At first, he had counted the hours that he didn't hear from the bank; then the days. He hoped that no news was good news: *it must have been accepted.* If only he could access their online account, he would know for sure whether it showed as a legitimate deposit; but Cath dealt with all that.

Before he had summoned the courage to explain the matter to Cath (he had serious doubts she would see his bold move as the stroke of genius he considered it), before he had a chance to ask her to do her internet banking thing to see if they were a hundred quid better off, before *that*, they received a phone call. What's more, which was just *typical*, it had to be *Cath* who answered the phone.

"Bob! Here! It's the bank! They say there's a problem with a deposit or something! I told them we haven't done any deposits! Maybe it's a scam!" Reluctantly, Bob followed his wife's hard-to-miss, increasing-in-volume yells. She was pacing the kitchen with the hands-free house phone. Her narrowed eyes were laden with suspicion. "They want to speak to you." She plonked the phone in his hand then stood with her arms folded, watching him.

Reluctantly, Bob put the phone receiver to his ear. He had his story all ready. He figured they could easily track him to the bank hole-in-the-wall at the supermarket where the deposit had been made; they would be certain to have a surveillance camera pinned on that, which would also tell them the exact time he made the deposit, which was undoubtedly time-stamped on the bank's records too. He hoped Cath would let him tell his story without screaming the place down in the background.

"Hello?"

"Mr Robert Gordon Geddes?"

"Yep. That's me, love."

Cath rolled her eyes. *Trust Bob to try the charming act.* A phoney deposit into their bank account on the Saturday that Bob did the shopping? How could she have been so stupid not to immediately suspect he would try something! The old fool!

"Date of birth? What d'you need that for? You gonna send me a birthday card?" Bob laughed.

Cath seethed. "Just do what they say," she hissed.

Bob complied and continued the security checks, that, while he joked that they were hardly necessary since they'd already spoken to his wife, were completed anyway. Then onto the details.

"Saturday the second of May, 1907 hours," Bob repeated the details the female voice related. "Well, if you say it was then, I must have made the deposit then, mustn't I?"

The kitchen door slammed behind him, and Bob flinched. He hoped the sound hadn't carried through the phone receiver, but at least Cath wasn't going to shout at him from the background.

"I know it sounds daft, but I found that banknote! Couldn't believe my luck! It blew through the fence into the garden! Might have come from next door – we've got a pretty weird neighbour" (this was the mildest thing he could think to call Amanda since they had learned of her subterfuge) "but I wasn't going to question it, and since it landed on my property, it's mine in law, right?"

The woman on the phone sounded faintly sympathetic. "I'm afraid it's not that straightforward, sir. And unfortunately, the banknote you tried to deposit is fraudulent which is a serious matter we need to…"

"Wait! What do you mean it was *fraudulent*? It wasn't stolen, was it?"

"The police will deal with whether the banknote was involved in a crime, but it was a fake note that you tried to pay into your account."

"*Fake?*" Bob sighed dramatically. "I might have *known* it was too good to be true! I was going to buy Caff – that's my wife – something special. She hasn't been well through this virus-thing – I thought it would cheer her up. Oh dear, oh dear! What happens now? Am I in trouble? You going to report me to the police? Lock me up?" His voice was convincingly tremulous and his chuckle suitably nervous.

"Nothing like that, sir," the official quickly reassured. "We follow protocol and always report fraudulent banknotes to the police, but…"

Bob sighed heavily. "Oh dear, oh dear," he repeated. "What have I got into now? And all I wanted was to buy Caff a little something!"

"Obviously, we can't credit your account with one hundred pounds, sir, and the police may want to hear how you came across the banknote. But other than that, the bank will consider the matter closed."

When Bob touched the button to end the call, Cath opened the door and came back into the kitchen. The timing was too exact to be coincidence; Bob assumed she had been listening at the door. To his surprise, she didn't go ballistic; she crossed her arms and glared at him. That steady, silent stare was bad enough though, and at last Bob said, "Aren't you going to say anything?"

She shrugged. "Well, I don't believe for a minute you were going to buy me *something special*, and it's nothing new that you're an old fool, but…" she sighed. "It seems that we're both landed in it with this money. I never should have agreed to look after it."

Bob shrugged, relieved that they weren't going to fight. "It's too late to go back, love, we need to decide what to do next. At least we now know the banknotes are fake."

"Do you think *all* of the notes are fake?"

Bob shrugged. "Who knows? But my guess? Yeah, it is."

Cath was perplexed. "But what was their game, then? I heard them say they had taken it from this man, Terry, and that Terry might have killed that woman for it! Why would he murder someone for *fake* cash?"

Bob suggested, "Maybe *he* didn't know it was fake. Or he was going to use it anyway – you know, fraud. Or maybe this geezer, Terry, is playing his own game – stringing them along and letting them think they've got one up on him!"

Cath was silent.

Bob was confident. "I think we wait. Those women don't know that it's fake, do they? They think they might get *murdered* over it! Let 'em stew. That's the least we can do after what they've put us through! No one is likely to come looking for the money here, are they?"

In the end, Cath went out. She took Cable and, leaving Bob to rant and rave and plan as unpleasant a demise as possible for their neighbours (knowing this capital crime was unlikely to happen), she walked down the road towards Torrdara Forest. When she reached the forest, she let Cable off his leash. *What a lot of angst there had been over nothing! The money was fake after all!*

Cath was tired of the whole business; tired of her wonderings about what was right and wrong about it, when it didn't matter anyway. *Might they still be charged with receiving stolen goods or profiting from a crime or fraud or some such thing?*

The May sun shone through the trees, dabbing light here and there on the forest floor. A familiar border collie dashed towards Cable and the two dogs milled around each other, mutually pleased. Coming towards her through the trees, following Peter, was Emily Wilson. She smiled when she spied Cath; it was quite heart-warming to meet a neighbour who seemed genuinely pleased to see her.

Pleasantries exchanged, they began to walk along the path together and Cath suddenly blurted, "I still remember that story you told about the Bible, that time we were all in the field. Sometimes I wish some of it was even true."

Emily looked across at Cath. "Why don't you think it's true?"

Cath shrugged. "Lots of reasons."

"Such as?"

"Well, science has disproved God!"

"How?"

Cath shrugged again. "You know, the Big Bang and evolution proves that God doesn't exist."

Emily shook her head. "But that's not true. There is no fact or scientific theory which disproves God. Science relies on observation and experiment to understand the physical world. Where there's lots of evidence and you can observe things behaving in exactly the same way again and again, you can prove whether something's true. Where there's much less evidence or you can't experiment, there are unproved theories. Some of the theory of evolution – like the ability of species to adapt in a limited way to their environment – you can prove because it happens now, and you can observe it; other parts *can't* be proved – like species evolving into another species."

"I suppose you *don't* think that monkeys turned into humans, then," interjected Cath.

"No," Emily agreed. "Species changing into different species has *never* been observed, so it's purely theoretical. You can't observe the start of the world – and although they've tried, no scientist has ever recreated this process. Besides, you would have to start with nothing, which is a pretty tricky experiment!"

Cath flicked a fly off her sleeve. "Well, I don't know all the details, of course, but leading scientists tell us that's what happened, and we'd be daft not to believe the experts!"

Emily remarked, "Leading scientists also say that the world shows every evidence of being designed, and some of *those* also believe in God."

"*Real* scientists believe that?!"

Emily smiled at Cath's incredulous tone. She picked up the tennis ball that Peter had dumped at her feet and threw it into the trees. "*Real* scientists," she repeated. "Plenty of scientists and other academics believe that there must be a designer or originator of the world. In fact, some believe in God because they *can't* credit chance, the Big Bang, evolution, and such with producing the incredibly intricate universe we live in. So, you can't really decide about God based on what scientists think, you'd need other evidence instead."

There was a pause in which Cath bent to pick up the ball that had been quickly returned by Peter. Peter was watching it intently, joyful when it was thrown, haring helter-skelter down the path with Cable close behind. At last Cath said, "I guess it's each to their own. You've got your way, I've got mine. As long as we're happy…" She didn't sound convincingly happy about her own chosen way, and she seemed to realise it as she quickly added with a laugh, "well, as happy as we can be, anyway!"

Emily kicked a pinecone from the path. "But belief of any kind should surely be based on evidence; we can choose to believe anything we like which might appeal to us or make us feel happy, but if we know that it isn't based on the truth, we'll never be really satisfied."

Cath chuckled. "It's funny to hear a religious person talking about *evidence*! I always thought they steered well clear of any proof and blindly hoped for the best!"

Emily was also amused. "When you look at the abundance of design in the world, you would think that evolutionists are the ones ignoring the evidence!"

"Touché," said Cath with a smile. "Well, perhaps we should agree that creation and evolution theories are *both* guesswork! Maybe we can't be sure about anything!" They reached a fork in the path and Cath gestured to the trail that led towards Kinbackie. She was walking further, she said, she might even go as far as Kinbackie. She was genuinely sorry that Emily had to turn back; debating their opposite worldviews distracted her from the whole sorry mess about the money. At least for a while.

CHAPTER 15

Wednesday 6 May 2020 continued

It seemed there was no escaping the problem of the money. Cath hadn't finished her favourite *Antiques for All* TV show that afternoon when the phone rang.

"You might remember me," said the man on the phone. "I did door-to-door visits when we were investigating your neighbour's death."

Silently, Cath handed the phone to Bob.

Bob hadn't remembered the name, DS Ian Prentice, but he could picture the tall young man who had stood at their front door, and who had subsequently seen him in Torrdara Forest. He struck Bob as a conscientious officer, a bit polished and la-de-da, with not much humour about him.

"What can I do for you, young man?" Bob asked jocularly.

Cath rolled her eyes. Always, *always* Bob thought he could charm his way through anything or wriggle out of trouble through his I'm-just-a-silly-old-man act. She grudgingly admitted that it often worked, but would their luck run out? The way things were going, they would be lucky to walk away from this money debacle breaking even – no better off than they had been before, but no *worse off* either.

"We've received a report regarding a fraudulent banknote you discovered on your property and that you subsequently tried to bank. I'm wondering if you could tell me what happened, Mr Geddes?"

It wasn't a question. He may as well have said *'you will now tell me exactly what happened, or we won't be having this polite phone conversation, we'll be interrogating you.'*

Bob managed a put-on, slightly nervous laugh. *Here comes the silly-old-man act*, thought Cath. "Can't believe I messed up," he said. "I thought there would be no harm in banking it, thought it was mine since it was in my garden. Didn't know it was fake! Might've known it was too good to be true!"

DS Prentice wasn't as quickly understanding as the lady from the bank had been. He listened in silence and there was no smile in his voice when he said, "Could you describe exactly where you found it, Mr Geddes?"

Bob was uncertain. He couldn't remember what he'd told the lady from the bank.

"We've got that square-type wire fencing, I think they call it chicken-wire or maybe it's rabbit-wire or something!" He was right about Ian Prentice not having a sense of humour. He didn't join in Bob's chuckle.

"Are you saying it was caught in the wire fence?"

"Not exactly … more like…" Bob was trying to imagine if it was possible for a banknote to blow through *and* remain stuck on the fence. No, that wouldn't make sense. Surely it would blow through and maybe be caught by a tree? "I'm saying it came through the gap in the fence and was caught up against a tree trunk on my side."

Ian Prentice interrupted. "Which fence are you referring to, Mr Geddes?"

"The side fence with the weird neighbour!" He attempted to lighten the tone again.

"Which side is…?"

"Witch!" Bob laughed loudly. "You've got that right! It was the witch's side alright! You know, the weird one! You can't have forgotten *her*!"

Yet again, Cath rolled her eyes, but this time Bob's attempt at humour got a smile in the tone. Apparently, the officer remembered Amanda-what's-her-name, with her black hair and eerie eyes. "I need you to verify which neighbour, Mr Geddes. We're not allowed to take guesses about who's weird and who's a witch."

"Lucky you," said Bob, pleased with the reaction. "I'm talking about the fence between us and Amanda-something." He'd hoped for another smile in young Prentice's tone, but this boy was good at self-control. Whatever he thought about Amanda, he wasn't going to reveal it.

"Amanda Finnes," Ian confirmed.

"Is that her last name?"

Ian observed, "Your boundary with Ms Finnes is quite overgrown."

"So what? It still came through her fence!" He was bold and blustering now, determined to stick to his story – and to make it stick. "Look, I know it sounds unlikely, son…"

Cath mentally groaned. *Bob would insist on patronising the police!*

"But sometimes unlikely things just happen! I thought it was my lucky day! I didn't know it was fake, of course!"

"I'm afraid you should still have handed it in. Technically, keeping found cash is a crime known as *theft by finding*. It's still theft."

"I'm not a technical man!" Bob chortled.

"Have you found any more banknotes?"

Bob laughed. "You've got to be joking! You think there are more hundred notes blowing around out here? It's the most exciting thing that happened for the last hundred years in these parts! Reckon it's the first, and probably the last one, I'll ever see!"

"If you do find any others, please let me know immediately. You've got my contact details?"

"I expect Caff has them on that card you left. CAFF?"

'Caff' ignored him. Bob pretended to note the number the detective recited. He didn't intend to ever be in touch.

"One last question, Mr Geddes, do you know a local man named Terry Vass?"

"Terry? Vass? Nope, don't think so. Think the only Terry I knew was a woman. It's one of those gender-thingy names, isn't it? I expect we'll all have to have them soon!" Bob laughed heartily and Cath groaned inwardly. *Trust Bob to find a way to be so insensitively un-PC with the police!*

On the whole, Bob thought his brush with the young officer had gone fairly well; so far as he could tell, DS Prentice was satisfied with his account.

But he didn't like the question about this Terry Vass. He must be the man the women were mixed up with, the one who might have killed the other woman who lived close by. If the money was fake, the sooner they got rid of it, the better.

***

Ian hesitated to click 'send' on his email. He had the green light from his boss and also from Tracey Redding, the NCA case contact. *But would it be enough?* He rocked back in his chair. Would four pieces of circumstantial evidence convince the Procurator Fiscal there were grounds to grant a search warrant for Bob and Cath Geddeses' house and premises?

Bob Geddes' criminal record made interesting reading. There were convictions for fraud and embezzlement. There were other charges and fines for more minor infractions – plenty of dubious dealings which had been investigated by Trading Standards over the last thirty years – and an investigation into two other money laundering offences: tax evasion and bribery. Bob had clearly enjoyed a colourful career, and although his criminal convictions were in his youth and thirty years in the past, his more minor offences and Trading Standards investigations were not. At the very least, it formed a picture of someone who might be mixed up with a large sum of illegal money.

Then came the report from the bank of a fake banknote deposited in Mr Robert Geddes' bank account. Ian wasn't remotely convinced by Bob's explanation.

Add to that the sighting of Bob Geddes close to the cottage connected to Terry Vass, and possibly to the missing money.

But the final piece of evidence that Ian hoped would convince the Procurator Fiscal a search warrant was necessary was the anonymous report to the Crimestoppers number last evening, which, since he had an interest in Strathavie, had been filtered down to him that afternoon. This time the caller had been female, and they reported a concern about stolen money being stored by *Cath Geddes* who lived in Torr, Strathavie.

Ian had left contact cards with all the Torr residents he had spoken to about Tanya Fletcher's death. Those cards also contained the anonymous Crimestoppers number. *Was it really going to be this easy to find the missing money?*

Ian sent the email.

CHAPTER 16

Thursday 7 May 2020

Peter, Emily Wilson's border collie, had never shown much interest in the trees at the back of the house. Now and again, he picked up an animal scent and followed his nose along the boundary, wagging his tail as if he would very much like to explore Hangman's Wood beyond. But, following an early morning commotion of excited barking which brought Emily to the kitchen window, Peter leapt the fence!

Emily put down her early morning coffee and rushed to the door. "Peter! PETER!" She gave his piercing whistle and was answered by another excited bark from the impenetrable jungle beyond her border.

Emily zipped up her warm jacket over her PJs and stuck her feet into her wellies. By the time she reached the fence, Peter was crashing through the trees towards her. He sailed over the fence, trailing twigs and leaves, and leaped around her in delight, wagging his tail in ecstasy, jubilant with his unexpected adventure. Half laughing, half scolding, Emily bent to pet him, then pulled at the paper he carried in his mouth. "What did you do, boy? What is this...? Open, Peter, open *now*."

She pulled the paper from his mouth, calling him to heel and heading back to the warm house. In the kitchen, she placed the piece of paper on the table. Although covered in dog saliva and grubby from the forest, it was nearly whole and perfectly discernible.

If she wasn't mistaken or going completely mad, it was a one-hundred-pound banknote!

***

Ian was sincerely glad that the other neighbour who had mysteriously discovered a rare banknote was not Amanda Finnes, with her creepy propensity to think they had a telepathic link or special relationship, but rather lovely Emily Wilson. She was a member of the local church Colonel Urquhart was also part of, and, since she had mentioned the matter to him, the Colonel joined them when Ian met Emily at her home. The Colonel was as intrigued as Emily was inclined to be amused.

A stiff breeze blew the dirty, black-brown clouds accumulating on the horizon higher into the sky and towards the strath. It did *not* feel like May; the day was borrowed from the distant winter. They remained outside, however, sticking to social distancing rules as well as they could, and Ian discarded his mask.

"I didn't know who to contact in the police, which is why I phoned the Colonel. I assume it's a joke," Emily said as Ian examined the banknote. "Toy money or something? Perhaps lost by a child in the wood…?" Her uncertainty was clear. Were there even such things as toy, relatively authentic-looking, one-hundred-pound Scottish banknotes? Not that she would know what a real one looked like; she had never seen one before. But how could one – real or fake – be lost in the tangle of Hangman's Wood?

"It's unlikely local children go anywhere near that wood. There's a local rumour that it's haunted, and it's so overgrown it would be pretty hard to walk through." The Colonel gestured to the dense woodland just beyond Emily's boundary.

"I was expecting it to be fake." Ian held the note up to the light, and then once more felt over it with his gloved fingers. "The other one that was, uh, discovered in the area…" He glanced towards Bob Geddes' house that he was now even more anxious to search. "The other banknote found close by *was* fake. We traced it to a batch sold on Amazon as theatre props."

Emily was incredulous. "That's allowed?"

Ian nodded. "It's perfectly legitimate. Someone might have simply ordered a batch – for whatever reason, kid's party or magic tricks or theatre show – and a few got loose in this area. Of course, one-hundred denomination notes aren't easy to spot as fakes – most of us don't routinely see them. But they're easy enough to spot in the retail and banking world. For starters, they might have 'Sold by Amazon' or a disclaimer about not being legal tender printed on them somewhere."

Emily laughed.

"So, that's the explanation!" The Colonel sounded relieved. He had begun to wonder if something far stranger was going on in the neighbourhood, especially since his previous conversation with Ian about a large sum of money in the area.

Ian frowned. "I can't see any disclaimer on this note, however, and I think I'd like another opinion." He knew that sometimes fake banknotes were used on the outside of a bundle to conceal the real ones beneath. Not for any good reasons, of course; it was only useful if you had stolen or illegitimate cash to hide. He walked to Emily's boundary with Hangman's Wood. It provided a convenient link between all the houses connected with the various incidents in Strathavie – convenient especially if you wished to remain concealed.

The Colonel joined him at the boundary. "A couple of years ago, they installed hidden cameras in the wood to monitor local pine martins. I don't know if they're still operable but I believe it was a wildlife charity who operated them on behalf of the local

Community Council. It's probably a long shot that the cameras would capture anything of interest to you, but..."

Ian nodded. "Definitely worth checking," he said. Turning back to Emily he asked, "Have you noticed any other unusual disturbance in the wood recently?"

"Peter barked at the crack of dawn earlier this week, Monday or Tuesday, I think. It was unusual but I didn't think much of it. There are occasional voices, especially since lockdown – one of the neighbours uses the wood as a shortcut to meet others in the field. They exercise their dogs together."

"Do you know who?"

"Lisette Simmons. She has a large dog called Monty and she sometimes meets with Cath and Amanda," Emily nodded in her neighbours' direction. "I think Lisette and Amanda work from home. They get together in the evenings."

Cath Geddes. Amanda Finnes. And now, Lisette Simmons.

It might pay to chat to Lisette Simmons and ask what she'd seen. He hadn't visited the houses north of Hangman's Wood, closer to Molly Johnson's cottage, when he interviewed locals about Tanya Fletcher's death.

Perhaps it was time that he did.

***

Cold from an early walk with Cable, Cath had completed a pilates workout, enjoyed a long, hot bath, got dressed in her comfiest leggings and sweatshirt, and then Bob returned from somewhere outside and interrupted her daily soap opera on TV.

"The police are next door! That young officer what's-it who came here and then phoned up about the banknote. I recognise his voice!" he said.

"At Amanda's?" Cath looked up eagerly. "I hope they arrest her!"

"Not Amanda's – the other one!"

"Emily? *Emily?* Are you sure? I wouldn't have thought she would be mixed up in anything!"

"I couldn't hear much," admitted Bob, and Cath noticed pine needles and foliage sprinkling his shoulders and dropping onto her clean floor. *He'd been standing at the boundary with Emily's house, trying to listen. Was this also to do with the money?*

As soon as he heard the car leave the house next door, Bob went to see Emily. Emily couldn't ask him in, so he stood at her doorstep plying her with questions. He ascertained that she had found a one-hundred-pound banknote which the police had taken to check its authenticity; she had been informed that another note that had been found close by – which Bob assumed was his note – was a banknote sold on Amazon for theatre productions and such. On this revelation, a mortified red tinge began to creep up Bob's neck. He hardly heard Emily's comment that the police had yet to verify whether the banknote she had found was real. Sleet began to fall; Bob made the weather his excuse and beat a hasty retreat.

"It's those women! Amanda-what's-it next door and the other one! I reckon they've played us like fools all along! Bought fake money on Amazon and spun a tall tale! That old lady who died couldn't have done *that*! *She* couldn't shop on *Amazon*! It's that witch next door…" His rant continued; his fury spilled over into extravagant, foul language as he decried Amanda and Lisette in every possible derogatory term– and that was too good for them in Cath's opinion too.

Cath wasn't as certain that Amanda or Lisette had instigated the whole thing though. *What would be the point of playing an extravagant practical joke by planting fake money bought on Amazon on them?* She still felt that the case of money originated at, or at least near, Molly's, and that they had taken it from this man, Terry, perhaps not knowing it was fake. However the story originated, the unpalatable truth was still mortifying. There was no treasure hoard. There was no case to even interest the police (unless it was Bob trying to cash a fake note, and it seemed they weren't going to pursue that). There was surely nothing illegal about toy banknotes sold on Amazon, and who would bother pressing charges for stolen toy money? But there was small comfort in that.

CHAPTER 17

Ian hadn't expected any special revelation from the banknote he had collected from Emily Wilson. Despite the fact that the missing cash purported to be in Strathavie consisted of one-hundred-pound Scottish banknotes, and although he knew that Bob Geddes' fake banknote might be explained by the occasional practice of inserting fake notes at the top of a bundle to conceal stolen or fraudulent money, it seemed unlikely that he had stumbled across evidence of the missing money the NCA were searching for.

The Police National Database stored information pertaining to police investigations that did not lead to any further action, or that remained unsolved. Since 1999, the database stored, by serial number, each stolen banknote where the serial number had been known and recorded, for example, theft from a Post Office, or from a source such as a security van carrying cash, or an Automatic Teller Machine (ATM). It also recorded when and where the banknotes had been stolen, and any other information which was known, such as fingerprints recovered from the scene.

Prior to 1999, information was patchy. The current one-hundred-pound banknote issued by the Bank of Scotland dated to 1987. There were no records of those notes until the 1999 police system began to properly record thefts of notes by their unique serial number. Even from 1999, relatively few were recorded. One-hundred-pound notes weren't common enough to present many opportunities to those so inclined to filch them. Lower denomination notes were much more popularly stolen.

But incredible though it seemed, the serial number on the banknote that Emily Wilson – or rather, her dog – had discovered, was red flagged and assigned to *the active NCA case*. He had discovered a banknote from the stolen cash. Probably the rest of it was in Strathavie somewhere; *did Hangman's Wood conceal more evidence?* Likely Bob Geddes knew something about it; Terry Vass and Bob Geddes seemed unlikely accomplices, but suddenly anything was possible.

When Ian's search warrant was granted that same morning, Ian gathered his team and immediately returned to Strathavie.

***

Cath was irritable – *even for her*. It was the money. It didn't matter how many times he told her it would be alright – which Bob himself believed implicitly – she *kept on worrying*. About whether it was right or wrong, about the women and that they might tell the police, about the man, Terry, who might have killed a woman over the cash – which Bob now thought was ridiculous since the banknotes had proved fake. She was even weird about Bob looking at the money again. She'd gone ballistic when he said he might check it to see if he could spot the 'Made by Amazon' thingy sign on them, or if he could spot *any* real ones.

Bob went off to the local shop. He would check the money when Cath took Cable out. He picked up a newspaper, a chocolate bar for himself, a box of Cath's favourite biscuits, and some fire lighters because they were on special offer by the till. Social distancing was technically in place in the shop, but, because it was small and extremely cluttered, nobody took much notice. Elspeth was in good spirits. She chatted almost non-stop about anything and everything and produced the most astounding facts about the Covid pandemic, most of which bore no resemblance to reality.

"Plenty of people coming out here breaking the rules!" Elspeth was saying. "*Three* cyclists passed just now, all in a line, *not one metre* between them! Did you hear about the money, Brian? I don't think you were here when I told the others." She switched track with dizzying speed, spearing Bob, whom she regularly miscalled Brian, with a swift glance.

Casually, Bob asked, "Money?"

"A *one-hundred-pound banknote*!" exclaimed Elspeth. "Emma – is it Emma? – lives close to you, she found one!"

"What, a *real* banknote?"

Elspeth chuckled. "Of course, it's real! The police took it away and examined it to make sure! You don't think there are *fake* notes wafting around Strathavie?" The other two listeners laughed too, and Bob managed a realistic sound of amusement. *If only they knew…*

Bob hoped the shock – and excitement – he felt wasn't evident. He laughed again. It was meant to sound light-hearted, but in his own ears it sounded harsh and forced. "I wonder if there's more!"

They all laughed again.

He paid for his paper and went straight home. *Were some of the banknotes real after all? He must examine that money!*

***

Knowing the cash was fake – made on Amazon or some such nonsense – it was all the more surprising for Cath to find three police officers at her front door. Two were in uniform, one was the same young sergeant that had visited previously.

Bob was still at the local shop. Cath barely glanced at the search warrant the sergeant offered her; she barely listened to the explanation he gave about the Covid regulations they would abide by throughout their search. She let them in with a curt, "Go ahead." Then she settled in her recliner to watch her favourite *Antiques for All* show on TV.

"Caff!" Bob was back from the shop. "What's happening, Caff?!"

In as few words as possible, she told him the police had a search warrant. They had just started in the garage. She turned up the volume on the TV, blocking out all Bob's exclamations and at last heard him stomping off to the garage. Everything that happened lately was connected to that wretched money. She no longer cared.

Let them search.

Pushing her chair further back, she snuggled deep into it and focussed exclusively on the TV. What will be ... would happen very shortly.

Once her show had ended, she was unable to resist the scene in the garage. Bob stood in the connecting doorway which linked the garage to the house. His expression was eloquent, but he didn't say anything and stood back so that she could join him and watch. The officers had almost completed their search. It hadn't taken long: the garage had plenty in it, but they were mostly large objects without too many obvious places of concealment. The most predictable hiding place behind and beneath pots of paint and odds and ends had already been thoroughly searched.

An officer noticed Cath. "We're keeping things as tidy as we can, Mrs Geddes."

Cath shrugged carelessly. "What do you think you'll find?"

"I reckon it's to do with that money I found, Caff," said Bob. "I told them it was a mistake. I thought I was allowed to keep it. It could happen to anyone!"

"I can't imagine they're searching to find more *fake* money!" She looked at the young detective who had been to their house before and was becoming a regular feature in their lives.

Ian was intrigued with Bob Geddes' reaction to the search. His face had been a study in anxiety. His ease only returned the further they looked – and came up with nothing. "There's a sum of money missing which the police are trying to trace," Ian said briefly.

"*Real* money? Not fake, like I found?"

"I told you they wouldn't search for toy money!" said Cath.

"No telling what the police will do these days," Bob retorted amicably. He was definitely improving in spirits as the search progressed.

When they finished their search, they were empty handed.

As the door shut behind the police officers, Bob turned to Cath. When and how Cath had removed the incriminating case, Bob had not the faintest idea. But that she had saved the day there could be no doubt.

"What did you do with it, Caff?"

Cath stared at him defiantly. "I got rid of it a few days ago."

No wonder she hadn't been keen for him to take another look! Bob had torn feelings. On the one hand, it was a stroke of genius that Cath had got rid of the case; on the other, at least some of the banknotes were real!

"Where did you put it?"

Cath nodded towards the fringe of Hangman's Wood they could see from their kitchen window. "In there," she said.

***

While the other officers returned to Aberlochee once they'd finished executing the search warrant, Ian decided to re-visit Molly Johnson's cottage and make enquires at Lisette Simmons' house. She and someone listed as Ken Wainwright had been living in rented accommodation in Torr since February, shortly before lockdown. That was also about the time the money the NCA had been tracking was last seen vanishing into Strathavie; but there was nothing necessarily suspect about *that*.

Ian had already clocked where Lisette Simmons lived relative to Molly Johnson's cottage; she was within easy reach of the Geddeses, Amanda Finnes, and Tanya Fletcher. Hangman's Wood provided a handy shortcut between them.

A middle-aged man opened the door at Lisette Simmons' house. He was balding, bland and uninspiring. Lisette was out walking the dog, he said. He wasn't sure where she had gone or when she would be back. "She often heads through the wood." Ken Wainwright gestured tiredly to the giant pines that clustered thickly on the other side of the road. He showed almost no interest in why the police might want to question his girlfriend. As soon as he could, he shut the door. Ian could hear the TV on loudly in the background and imagined Ken already snoozing in front of it.

He went on to Molly Johnson's cottage. All appeared as he and the Colonel had last left it. When he emerged from the entrance to the cottage, he spied a woman and a large dog appearing from Torrdara Forest Walk. When he introduced himself, Lisette Simmons seemed faintly amused.

"The rumours are not exaggerated," she said.

Ian didn't ask for an explanation. He was trying to imagine how such a vivacious woman could be the girlfriend of such a weary man. She positively sparkled in comparison.

"Do you know a man called Terry Vass?"

She appeared more interested than concerned. "I know *of* him," she said. "I wouldn't say that I knew him well personally."

She glanced quickly towards her house, clearly visible from where they were standing. *Was she worried about something?*

"What do you know *about* Terry Vass?"

She shrugged. "He's connected to the old lady who lives – I should say *lived* – there, where you've just come from." She nodded at the entrance to *Cois Dara* and Ian wondered how long she had observed him. *Had she watched him from the forest?* "Other than that, I don't know much. A friend of mine had a fling with him and was very hurt when he broke it off. She's the type that gets used by men like Terry – at least, men with Terry's reputation." She spoke candidly and yet Ian wasn't sure it was the whole truth. *Had Lisette also been involved with Terry?*

"What's your friend's name?"

"Her name? Well, I suppose it's alright to say – Amanda Finnes. She lives in Torr."

Ian nodded. *Amanda Finnes had a connection with Terry Vass.* He tucked the information away. "Do you know anything about a large sum of money – in high denomination banknotes – in connection with either Molly Johnson or Terry Vass?"

She laughed loudly. "Oh sorry!" she sobered up. "It's just sounds like a joke – the police looking for missing money, especially in a place like this!" She gestured around them, at the tranquil, deserted greenery. She chuckled again. The detective barely smiled; his dark eyes were hard to read. He *did* deserve his reputation.

"Have you ever discovered, or taken possession of, any one-hundred-pound Scottish banknotes?"

If Lisette was involved, she was very good at disguising it. "No! I only wish I had!" She called her large dog, Monty, away from digging a hole. Monty acted as though he didn't know his own name. In the end, she dragged him away and put on his leash. Ian watched her walk back to her home where Ken was probably already snoring by the telly.

He wondered what Lisette Simmons wasn't telling him.

***

Lisette watched from the front window of the house until DS Ian Prentice disappeared from view. "He's gone," she commented to Ken. "The police haven't found the money yet, so it's obviously no longer at the Geddeses'."

Ken was sat at a large screen – but not the TV that Ian had imagined. Instead, he was watching a clear camera image of Molly Johnson's cottage including the hotch-potch outbuildings and yard. "There's no sign of movement at the cottage. Anything else we should do?"

Lisette shook her head. "We wait," she said.

CHAPTER 18

It was Bob's first visit to Hangman's Wood. He didn't like the great outdoors and had no desire to explore its hidden depths, but any bias was forgotten in the urgent need to control the money. He explained to Cath that, at the very least, they should make sure it was still safely hidden; Cath had admitted to hiding it in a rush, and since the catch on the case was completely kaput since Bob's rough interference, the banknotes might escape their hiding place. Since Emily (or the dog) had discovered a banknote, Cath had an uneasy feeling about the remaining contents of the case.

Bob panted loudly as he tried to keep up with Cath's rapid steps along the faint path through the wood. Then, she suddenly changed direction and began ducking under branches as quietly as she could. She didn't want to rouse Emily's dog, Peter, who had barked the last time she had been there.

She halted abruptly.

An unintelligible exclamation reached Bob.

"What?" he demanded in a rough whisper. "*What?*"

Cath remained silent. When he pushed aside the last low branch and reached her, Bob saw it too.

Stark against the dark, earthy forest floor, were banknotes scattered far and wide.

It *must* have been animals. A dog, deer, badgers? A person would surely have carried off the money – but someone could definitely discover the hoard of cash now. While there was little wind gusting through the thicket, a breeze had already spread the notes around.

Bob and Cath picked up all the banknotes they could find, scouring the confined tangled undergrowth, uncomfortable and dirty, with prickly twigs tearing at their clothes. Cath forgot about ticks and other insects. They both forgot about anything but the need to gather the evidence, and then they could decide what to do. They tried to remain silent through their searching and not alert Peter, about whose presence Cath had also warned Bob.

When they had collected all the notes they could, they crouched on the forest floor and put them back in bunches, securing them with elastic bands. Bob counted them as best he could. They didn't total one million pounds, but they'd never counted them before and couldn't be sure precisely how many were in each stack. They placed them in a strong plastic sack, reinforced with other layers of plastic sacks that Bob had brought for that purpose; then they added some of the untouched bundles from the briefcase to the stash. Reluctantly, Bob left one pristine wad of banknotes in the case. They carefully buried the plastic sack of notes in the forest floor and pushed and shoved a large branch on top. Cath scattered leaves and pine needles over it so it didn't appear disturbed; Bob, panting heavily and covered in sweat, looked carefully around their hiding place.

He picked up the incriminating case with its one valuable wad. Cath shook her head. Of all the components of Bob's master plan, this was the craziest part. Although, it *was* just possible that planting the buckled case containing a stack of notes back in an outbuilding at Molly's cottage *might* distract the police – and this man Terry – and cause them to look in another direction.

Cath didn't think Bob noticed the banknotes she had stuffed in her own pocket. She felt insects and twigs and who-knows-what all over her and wanted nothing more than to soak in the bath and remove the grime of her latest experience in the wood. Then she planned a leisurely lunch, finished off with a large latte and a big slice of the banana loaf she so enjoyed. She would put up her feet and enjoy it while she watched the telly.

And, for a while, forget about the money.

CHAPTER 19

Sunday 10 May 2020

Bob clambered out of bed before dawn. It was a dark, lowering morning with a thick covering of unfriendly clouds. Bob collected the case, called goodbye to Cath who lay unmoving in bed, and left the house.

Cath calculated the time it would take Bob to walk to Molly Johnson's cottage, leave the case and one wad of cash, and return. Bob was hopeful that Terry would find the note he had also enclosed. Cath didn't know about the note which denounced the two women who had stolen the money – it seemed to Bob the least he could do after that note they'd written to him.

As soon as Bob left, Cath dressed and hurried out into the dark morning. Softly, she entered her neighbour's driveway and, as quietly as she could, headed for Amanda's shed. The shed was locked, which was a pity, but it was a minor hiccup in her plan. As Cath was well aware, an open lean-to adjoined the shed; she could plant the banknotes she had secreted in her pocket in there.

Feeling inspired, Cath kept a few back and put one in a tree, stuck one half under the shed door, scattered a generous sprinkling over the front hedge next to the road, and feeling daring, she crept up to the front door and placed one half under the door mat, and another in a horrible artificial tree close by.

She felt like an artist as she viewed the litter she had left behind; the stiff breeze that was beginning to blow down the strath would probably help, not hinder, spreading the money around Amanda's dwelling and out into Torr. *What would the police make of that?*

Cath returned to the house feeling almost light-hearted. Although she hadn't shared her plans with Bob, he would probably enjoy it as much as she had. So far as she was concerned, the only money that remained was now back at Molly's cottage or safely buried in the wood.

***

Amanda had had a bad morning: a *very* bad morning. Not only had she woken earlier than usual after a later than usual night (she was feeling inspired to write and had drafted two chapters of her novel in the early hours of the morning), but she was also worried about Terry's briefcase. The police had searched her neighbours, hadn't they? But they didn't seem to have found the money! Was Terry still out there hunting for it? *Did he suspect her?*

When she left the house to buy a Sunday paper and extra paracetamol for the headache she knew was coming, she almost collapsed. She didn't need to examine each individual piece of litter sticking out of her hedge, dancing across her driveway and waving to her from the bottom of her doormat. She just knew.

Terry's banknotes!

It must have been Cath. What had she discovered about the cash? Had she also informed the police about the money now strewn like confetti around her driveway? *What about Terry?*

She placed a frantic call to Lisette, leaving her a jumbled voicemail message since her fingers were shaking too badly to type a word. Still trembling, she began to frantically collect all the notes, horrified as she at last discovered the woodpile strewn with cash, some of which had escaped their hiding place and were joyously exploring her back garden. *How far afield had they travelled?* As she watched, one soared high on the breeze and vanished into Sid and Edith's garden.

By the time Lisette arrived, the money had been contained. Lisette had brought Monty with her and was as unflappable as ever. They should take the money Amanda had collected and return it to Molly's cottage. Then forget about it all. Forget it had ever happened. Lisette decreed this as if simply *deciding* to forget made that impossible thing happen. She was acting as if there was nothing whatever to be worried about. Amanda began to suspect that Lisette intentionally made her feel stupid.

Amanda fetched Faroe and they both walked to Torrdara Forest as if it was an entirely normal thing to do with several thousand pounds of cash concealed on them. They made their way through the tangled undergrowth at the back of *Cois Dara* and reached the deserted yard of the cottage. The outbuildings were much as they were when, nearly three weeks previously, Amanda had removed Terry's hidden stash.

But, unless they were dreaming it, *the case was back*: broken, battered and soiled, but *definitely the same case!*

Inside it was a scribbled note which incriminated *them*.

***

When Cable ran eagerly to meet his erstwhile friend Monty, and Faroe waddled around the corner as fast as his short legs would carry him, Cath could see nowhere to hide. But then, why should *she* be the one trying to avoid *them*? They were bound to meet in such a small community. At least she a moment of warning, and when they faced her, she stood her ground.

"Hello!" exclaimed Lisette, as if nothing but pleasantries had ever passed between them.

Amanda was hiding behind her large sunglasses even though it was a cloudy day. She didn't seem well, and Cath had the slightest pang of conscience that she had caused that, before she quashed it and wished heartily that she'd planted banknotes at Lisette's house too.

"I take it you planted the money at my house?" Despite how unwell she appeared, Amanda managed a surprisingly fierce tone.

"Oh, that's right, that would be after *you* planted stolen cash on me!" retorted Cath. "Oh, and if that's not enough, you spin a lie about a poor old lady who *asked you* to look after it – instead of telling me that you're both involved with some dangerous criminal called Terry who's likely to murder anyone who has the money!"

For the first time since she had met her, Lisette had no ready answer; she seemed genuinely surprised. Cath focussed her anger on her; Amanda already seemed utterly defeated.

"And what exactly was *your* connection with *Terry?* Plenty you'd rather keep from your husband, I'll be bound!"

Lisette didn't answer that. Instead, she waved a scribbled note around. "Did you write this?"

"I don't know what you're talking about," snapped Cath. "I haven't written any notes…" She trailed off in sudden doubt. *Bob. He had mentioned landing the women in it with Terry. Trust him to add to his stupid plan!* But did that mean that Lisette and Amanda had found the case Bob returned? Perhaps they had just come from the cottage. Had they put the banknotes she'd spread around Amanda's there? *Or taken the ones Bob had left behind?* What weird coincidences were these?

Lisette was watching her. "What will you do now?" she asked casually.

"That depends on what *you* choose to do," Cath said stiffly, making it up as she went along.

"Could you return the rest of the money? Say no more about it?"

Cath shrugged, thinking of Bob. *Bob would never return it. And no one would ever find it.*

Lisette was waiting for an answer, but through the trees, crashing towards them was Emily's border collie, Peter, followed by Emily who was smiling cheerfully. Amanda waved a hand feebly and immediately left for home. She seemed about to collapse. Lisette clearly wanted to speak further but when Cath hailed Emily, she, too, reluctantly moved on.

***

"I hope I didn't interrupt anything," Emily said, once she was left alone with Cath.

Cath smiled grimly. "Nothing important."

Since you could have cut the atmosphere with a knife, Emily probably didn't believe her, but she didn't pursue it. "I think the last time we met we were talking here too!" Emily gestured around the forest, and Cath remembered the sunshine of that pleasant May day. Now a capricious breeze blew stiffly through the trees and clouds cluttered the sky; so far as Cath was concerned life had also taken a darker turn.

Was life meant to be like this? A purposeless existence, with chance happenings, meaningless twists and turns, then nothing?

They began to walk along the path together. Emily looked questioning. "I hope things are OK?"

"Humph…" Cath made a non-committal sound, then, "I suppose *you* don't despair that life is meaningless?" she asked drily.

Emily smiled at her tone. "No. I know it's not. Don't get me wrong, I have my off-days, but fundamentally I'm convinced that my life has purpose."

"Some secret religious-type knowledge, I presume."

"Not secret – it's in the bestselling book in the world!"

Cath laughed. "I guess you mean the Bible! It's seriously the bestselling book?!"

Emily nodded. "It seriously is! And it explains that life was created by God and has value and meaning and purpose."

Cath sighed. "Believing something like that is like positive thinking. It makes you *feel* good because you *think* there's a point to life. Of course, that doesn't make it *true*, but I can see why it makes you feel better."

Emily shook her head. "But what a person believes is only as good and as satisfying as the evidence it's based on, surely."

Cable and Peter careened around them, and Cath distractedly threw the ball that Cable urgently pressed into her hand. "You said that about evidence the last time we discussed this," she said. "Alright then, what evidence – I mean *real, actual* evidence that we both know about here and now – supports your view that God created the world?"

"Well, for starters, think what we know about ourselves," said Emily. This time she kicked the ball that Peter triumphantly flung at her feet, managing to send it some distance into thick heather; both dogs went full pelt after it. "Take the concepts of right and wrong," she continued. "Either there is a creator, who decreed right and wrong and instilled it into humans by giving us a conscience, or it's evolved through evolution and changes over time to suit current culture or whatever. So, a crime like murder or rape or paedophilia would only be wrong if the law of the land or current culture says it's wrong. But if it begins to suit the majority of people to legalise it and culture changes, then it's not wrong anymore. But we *know* that something like murder is *always* wrong because we're designed with that knowledge."

"Something like paedophilia is *always* wrong," Cath said emphatically. "It's disgusting!"

"Of course! But the point is that evolution doesn't logically lead to that point of view. If we're pointless, purposeless accidents and right and wrong evolves along with everything else, you can't say that anything is always wrong. But we instinctively know that a crime like paedophilia is always, at all times, absolutely *wrong* – because we're created with that knowledge."

They were momentarily distracted by the noise of the dogs pouncing and rolling and play-fighting in the heather. "Evolution concludes that we're no more valuable than they are," Emily nodded fondly at the two animals.

"I'm inclined to agree," Cath said lightly.

Emily smiled. "I get that – on one level. But we know that a human death is more tragic than that of ... well, say a pig or a slug! We act *against* the survival of the fittest in our protection of disabled, young, and vulnerable humans. It surely makes more sense that we're *designed* with these values; it doesn't make sense that they have *evolved* contrary to the theory of evolution, does it?"

Cath shrugged. "Perhaps that type of thing evolved because people found they were happier protecting others? Maybe it gave them a sense of purpose or something."

"Purpose!" Emily managed to sound shocked. "Whatever – or whoever – gave us the notion of purpose? Surely we should only be doing the bidding of our DNA!"[3]

Cath laughed. "I know you're quoting Richard Dawkins. I've read some of what he has to say."

Emily suggested, "I think we seek purpose in life because we're designed with the knowledge that it can be found."

---

[3] This is a reference to a quote by Professor Richard Dawkins: "DNA neither cares nor knows. DNA just is. And we dance to its music." — Richard Dawkins, River Out of Eden: A Darwinian View of Life.

"God again, I suppose! ... Cable! CABLE! NO!" Cath hauled her Labrador off the carcass of a well-decaying rabbit. Emily scolded Peter who was speedily gulping down a dubious morsel from the same carcass before he could be stopped, rather as if he feared a famine.

"Well, if the world has been created, what a mess it's in!" Cath gestured in disgust to the remnants of a once-living creature.

Emily nodded. She knew that Cath had already heard her thoughts about why things had gone so wrong in the world – when the first people chose their own way over their Creator's. "Why don't we prosecute whatever creature killed that animal?" she mused.

"Why indeed!" Cath re-joined. "But obviously wild animals don't know it's wrong to kill. They're simply surviving the best they can. They can't think the way we do."

"I'm afraid naturalistic thinking doesn't allow that you or I have a *mind*," said Emily. "It only admits to a brain because it only allows for physical elements. Animals have brains, of course, but we know that we have more than a brain – we have minds that make deliberate, moral choices for which there are consequences: if we commit murder, we're punished for it. The evidence about the human mind supports creation over evolution."

"Well, I admit I definitely have a mind!" said Cath.

Emily chuckled. "Better not admit that you *don't* have a mind, or I'll win the argument hands down!"

Cath laughed too. "I also admit that it's a strange paradox that the scientists who hold with naturalism and evolutionary-type-thinking don't admit to having a mind to do it with!"

"I guess they hope that no one will notice where their logic leads!" said Emily.

They slipped leashes back on the dogs as they exited the forest and began to walk the final stretch along the road to their homes, continuing their conversation.

As they parted, Cath commented, "I still don't see why God doesn't make it simple for us if He's really there. He could paint a neon sign across the sky every day so people can know for sure!"

"He wrote a Book which is full of evidence that can be investigated and tested and believed," said Emily.

"The Bible, of course!"

"Yes ... but to come back to your point, I think He doesn't go further and write signs across the sky and such because He wants our trust. He's given us *enough* evidence to seek Him and find Him – but He doesn't blast it across the sky for those who won't believe. Forcing someone to trust in you isn't real trust at all."

CHAPTER 20

Ian never anticipated that CCTV of pine martins would help solve an NCA case. But Monday morning found him watching video footage of the past two weeks – the Highland Pine Martin Watch charity didn't keep more than this – of two camera angles showing tree trunks, a dim forest clearing, and the tall waving branches of Scots pine trees. One advantage was that, with the correct ID and password, he could view the footage from his own desk; but three hours into fast-forwarded jerky movements of quiet woodland, his eyes were blurring over. He had delegated some days of the recording to junior colleagues, and at lunchtime the PC viewing footage from Sunday 3 May saw the curious sight of a woman crawling through the undergrowth at 7.47am and lying flat on the ground by a fallen tree trunk. The figure lay unmoving on the ground in the wood and after fifteen minutes crawled back through the undergrowth and out of sight.

There was one clear image of her face, when, unknowingly, she looked straight at the camera.

It was *Cath Geddes*.

Monday 4 May yielded another exclamation from another colleague. Early that morning, a woman came into view – *hauling a large, rectangular briefcase*. It seemed inconceivable that this *wasn't* the case containing the money. *How many other cases were there like this that someone would want to hide?* She was on and off camera without any evidence where she had gone, but this was it! *Cath Geddes had buried the case* – and Ian would have bet a significant amount that *she hadn't told her husband!* When they turned up with the search warrant the Friday of that week, the money was already safely in the wood!

With renewed hope, they scanned the next few days and on Saturday two figures came into view, by posture secretive and stealthy, struggling through the undergrowth, following the same route that Cath had taken previously. They disappeared from view; when they reappeared into camera view, Bob Geddes was carrying the case.

They had caught them!

The revelations began to unfold more quickly after that. Not only did they have a direct link with Bob and Cath Geddes and what seemed very likely to be the case which contained the missing cash, but Ian received a phone call from 'Uncle Sid' Segrave, who claimed he had found a one-hundred-pound Scottish banknote! Any other time, Ian wouldn't have treated this as priority but since it seemed likely to be yet another missing note, he set off to Torr on a double mission. He would visit Sid and Edith and interview Bob and Cath Geddes. If need be, he would bring the Geddeses in for questioning.

The first visit was easy. Sid and Edith were only sorry that they could not prolong the encounter with their favourite young man. They were eager to speculate on the cause of such unexpected treasure – perhaps bandits hiding in the area with their ill-gotten gains – and happily gave the banknote into Ian's keeping, certain he was on the verge of single-handedly solving a complex crime. "If anyone can do it, it's you, son!" said Sid heartily.

Edith nodded eagerly. "You bring those thieves to justice," she said solemnly.

Ian walked the short distance to the Geddeses' large home.

"You back again?" Bob greeted him jovially when he opened the door. Ian could smell delicious baking wafting from the house. "Come to search for more money?" teased Bob. If he was put out by Ian's appearance, it certainly wasn't apparent.

"No search warrant this time, Mr Geddes, but I would like to ask you some questions about a case of money."

"Why do you think I would know anything about a *case of money?*" scoffed Bob. "Because I found one banknote which wasn't even real? Caff? CAFF? You should come and hear this!"

"I'd like to speak to Mrs Geddes too," Ian agreed, as if it was his idea.

"It's about the money *again*," Bob explained. "Search again, if you'd like! You won't find anything!"

"I don't doubt it," said Ian. "But I would like to ask you why you both appear in CCTV images, captured in Hangman's Wood behind your house…"

Bob blurted, "They've got *cameras* in that old wood? What do they want cameras in there for?"

"Pine martins," said Ian drily; he didn't bother correcting Bob's incredulous exclamation of "they've got cameras to watch birds?!" although Cath muttered scornfully, "Pine martins aren't *birds*!"

Ian continued, "CCTV imagines of *you*, Mrs Geddes, carrying a large case into the wood. The case looks identical to the one we know is missing, and other images show you in the wood on other occasions, including Mr Geddes returning carrying an identical case on Saturday. Where did you put it, Mr Geddes?"

Bob didn't even try to prevaricate. "Back at that old cottage where it belongs!" he snapped. "Me and Caff wanted nothing to do with that cash. Two women neighbours spun a yarn about needing someone to look after it, to keep it safe from a man called Terry they were both mixed up with. Caff took it out of the kindness of her heart, and then the trouble began! We didn't know it was stolen or mixed up in crime! We put it in the wood because we didn't want any trouble, and then we decided we should put it back where the women said they got it from. That's it. That's all we've done – and good riddance, I say!"

It was such an extraordinary confession that it seemed likely to contain some truth, and it would be easy enough to prove at least some of the story. "So I'll find the case and all the money at Molly Johnson's cottage?"

Bob shrugged. "Should be there. Unless someone else has taken it – like those women again – Amanda and Lisette-something-or-other. Or that man they were trying to hide it from – Terry. I'll come with you, if you like."

Cath Geddes corroborated everything her husband said and, on the basis that it was better to keep Bob Geddes close by until he could verify his story, Ian agreed to his company.

Small talk with Bob Geddes wasn't difficult. Ian wouldn't trust him as far as he could throw him but there was no history of violence in his record; he was a crook, and there was bound to be more to the story than Bob admitted, but he wasn't objectionable as a companion. His views of the strath, Covid, Scotland versus England, women, his wife, and life in general were, in Ian's opinion, ignorant, but harmless enough.

At Molly Johnson's cottage, in the shed that had in recent days been padlocked, there was a buckled case.

It was empty.

There was no money.

CHAPTER 21

On the whole, Ian was inclined to believe that Bob Geddes' surprised reaction to the empty case was genuine. If appearances could be trusted, Bob had been expecting at least some banknotes to be there. All the way back to the Geddeses' house he tried to convince Ian that the money had definitely been in the case. When they reached the house, Bob was obviously hopeful that Ian would leave.

"It's as simple as that," he reiterated. "Nothing more to it – we put it back and now I've no idea *where* the cash is! But if I were you, I'd search over there!" With a sweep of his arm, he gestured to Amanda Finnes' house crouching behind the tall fir trees on his boundary.

Cath joined them at the door, her expression shuttered and by posture ready to close the door on Ian as soon as she could. But Ian was going nowhere. He was quickly losing patience with stories and excuses and what he strongly suspected were, at best, half-truths.

"You do understand that this is your last chance to tell the whole truth and possibly escape serious charges that may be brought against you if we subsequently find you have concealed, or had any part in concealing, stolen banknotes that were in the briefcase you placed at Mrs Johnson's cottage? You are now under caution…" Bob had heard the words before. He planted his feet and crossed his arms as tightly as he could across his generous girth. His eyes narrowed and he clamped his mouth tight shut.

"Anything you do say may be given in evidence," Ian concluded. "Do you understand?"

Bob cleared his throat. "Well enough."

"You understand that we have camera footage showing you both in the wood, with a case which we believe once contained a substantial amount of stolen money. If necessary, we will search the wood to find anything buried or concealed there, but it will certainly help you, especially considering the charges which may be brought against you, if you tell me the whole truth about the money now."

There was an icy silence while Ian waited. Then, "Tell it all, or I will, Bob," Cath said wearily.

Perhaps Bob was going to do that anyway. From his chequered past, he probably knew when he was beaten. "There's some money buried in the wood," he said. "We didn't know what to do with it, we weren't *definitely* going to keep it, we were just going to wait and see. I don't see why we shouldn't benefit from some of it since it's caused us so much trouble!"

Ian took a deep breath. *At last, they were getting somewhere.* "Right. I'd appreciate it if you could show me where it's hidden, and we'll take it from there." He forbore to point out that much of the *trouble* they had experienced from the money was of their own making. They could have brought the case straight to the police.

"Will we be charged?" Cath asked.

"We're the victims here!" Bob blustered. "Those women set us up! I hope you're going after them, *they* started all this, and I wouldn't be surprised to find they took their own share of the money!"

Ian smiled grimly. "Oh, we'll be questioning them alright," he said.

***

It was teatime in Torr and Amanda was writing an engrossing scene in her debut novel. The sun was already setting noticeably later; by mid-June, the sky would retain some light for most of the night. She wasn't sure when she first became aware of unusual sounds from the back of the house. She went to the kitchen window and saw the intriguing sight of a man and a woman in white paper suits. They exited the Geddeses' garden gate and entered Hangman's Wood. When she crept under the trees and peeped through the spy hole to the Geddeses' house, she could make out a couple of cars; one had police markings.

It must be about the money! It seemed unlikely that Bob or Cath had murdered the other and hidden the body in the wood. Although that might be a good scene for her book…

It was about the time the women used to meet and chat. Now, instead of innocuous chat about pandemic conspiracy theories and philosophical talk about the meaning of life, there were people in white overalls looking as if they were going to examine a crime scene. *How had one scene morphed into the other?*

She placed a chair by her patio doors and watched as the white suits reappeared carrying plastic bags. *Definitely more the bulk of banknotes than body parts.*

If the police knew Cath's part in the money saga, Cath certainly wouldn't spare telling them about her or Lisette.

How long before they came for her?

CHAPTER 22

Tuesday 12 May 2020

For the first time in what felt like *months*, Cath felt rested. She checked the calendar and was surprised to see that it was, in fact, only two short weeks ago that she had been chatting to her neighbours in the back field and had learned that Molly was dead. Two weeks of muddle and anxiety about a stash of illegal cash – concluding with her and Bob being considered for criminal charges.

Sergeant Prentice was quite optimistic about the charges though. They had cooperated with the police and, although somewhat late in the day, they had at least saved the police from searching Hangman's Wood. They had, initially, received money they didn't know was stolen – which might make a 'handling stolen goods' charge hard to stick. Bob had technically committed 'theft by finding' in keeping the banknote he had found; strictly speaking, he had also committed offences under the Forgery and Counterfeiting Act – including being in possession of, and using, a fake note. But again, there was the counter-defence that Bob had no idea it was fake. There were other potential charges, such as 'wasting police time' since they had lied about the money when they knew the police were searching for it; lying to the police could also be a more minor misdemeanour offence – but all-in-all, Sergeant Prentice felt their chances of escaping the more serious charges were fairly good.

Of course, there was still the matter of local reputation and what people would deduce from the rumours that were certain to circulate. Bob thought they could manage that pretty well too. "Once they learn those women probably had affairs with Terry-what's-it and stole his money, they'll have better things to talk about," he said. It was nothing to Bob whether this was actually true or the damage such gossip would do; so far as Bob was concerned, 'those women' deserved all that was coming to them.

And Cath agreed. People must suffer the consequences for the stupid things they did. That was the kind of ready justice you expected in life. If you got caught, you paid the consequences; if you didn't…

Was there really anyone else – like God – to whom people were ultimately accountable? *Surely not!* And yet, if not, what explained the apparent design of the universe? Or the way people thought and questioned and kept searching for spiritual answers?

During their walk along the final stretch of road last Sunday, Emily had mentioned this:

Where did non-material ideas, superstitions and such come from to start with; a physical brain alone couldn't account for them. Why didn't these ideas evolve away if the spiritual realm was proven to be non-existent and irrelevant to surviving as the fittest? Was it because people were designed with an awareness of another dimension, one that had to do with God?

How did environmental movements come about? Why would anybody bother to save the world for future, equally purposeless, futile, suffering people? Yet there were millions of people who wanted to preserve the world for those who would follow. Was it because people were designed with the knowledge that life was precious and meaningful?

The physical brain could explain the physiology of the eye, but not its appreciation of beauty; it could explain the physical act of hearing, but not the love of music; surely a mind was needed to explain these things.

And what about the mind-boggling genius of DNA — more complex than any computer program and absolutely impossible to have evolved?[4] What about other scientific evidence which fitted the creation story at least as well as, if not better than, evolution?

What if there really was *God?*

Well, at least the quandary about the money was over. In the end, they had been more victims than perpetrators. If God was real, He would surely take account of that.

***

Amanda told herself that she had been going to call the detective anyway, even without the unnerving police activity next door and in Hangman's Wood. Reluctantly, she reached for an old cake tin hidden behind odds and ends at the back of a kitchen cupboard. Inside the tin, crammed in disorderly fashion, were the banknotes she had taken from Terry's briefcase: the five thousand pounds he owed her, plus several thousand as 'compensation' for all the emotional damage and trauma he had caused her. She removed several of the banknotes and prepared to return Cath the same favour she had shown her.

She pushed the money through the thick foliage which separated their houses, and, sneaking out into the back field, she threw banknotes like confetti into the Geddeses' back garden and watched them flutter like ungainly leaves to the ground. They looked far bigger, and less discreet, than she had thought they would; in fact, they looked too stupidly obvious to be anything but deliberately planted. But it was too late to rethink her plan now.

---

[4] Many Christian scientists and apologists have commented on this — see resources suggested in End Matters at the end of the book.

She phoned the young officer who had left his card. Sergeant Prentice came immediately. He had been coming to talk to her that day anyway, he said, and Amanda knew why. *Cath had spilled the beans.*

A stiff breeze had sprung up when Ian, with a colleague, approached Amanda's front door. Her home didn't improve on acquaintance; to Ian, the ad hoc miscellanea of fake and real felt as distasteful as on his previous visit. Nor did Amanda herself become more palatable, despite the smile pasted on her face. There was something oddly unsettling about the woman. She got too close; she seemed to be searching for a kindred spirit in him that he knew she would never find except in her imagination.

Amanda focussed exclusively on Ian, ignoring the female DC who accompanied him. She felt she could see sympathy and understanding in Ian's dark eyes; she fancied he might be smiling at her beneath his mask.

"I've spotted some *banknotes* blowing about the garden next door!" she gushed. "I've thought there was something funny going on there for a while! If you ask me, Cath and her husband have been up to something fishy. I've heard that he's a criminal…"

If Ian was smiling it *didn't* show in his deadpan tone. "We've interviewed Mr and Mrs Geddes about money recently found in the area," Ian interrupted the flow. "When did you see banknotes in their garden?"

"Just now! Whatever they told you, I expect they've kept some to spend on themselves!"

Discovering more money in the Geddeses' garden, flapping around in the breeze looking ludicrously obvious, was an anti-climax. DC Rickshaw collected the notes she could see, with Bob and Cath calling their neighbour plenty of unrepeatable names from their back door.

"She must've planted them!" shouted Bob.

Ian cut through Bob's yelling and Amanda's shrill counteraccusations. He didn't believe that Bob Geddes was stupid enough to have kept some cash so insecurely it was miraculously blowing around his garden, especially with criminal charges currently being considered against him and Cath. He was tired of the ridiculous charade concocted by feuding neighbours who had complicated – if not compromised – a serious NCA investigation. Turning abruptly to Amanda, he asked, "If we examine these banknotes for fingerprints, will we find *yours* on them?"

Amanda's already washed-out features grew paler. *She had handled the banknotes in her home, never thinking she would have to return them. They would certainly find her fingerprints somewhere on them. How had she not thought of that?* She bunched her large cardigan around her middle as if she were literally holding herself together. Tears formed in her eyes.

Ian ignored her distress. "If you prefer, we can conduct this interview at the police station, but if you're happy to continue here, I would like to caution you with regards to anything you now say about the briefcase and the money we have recently discovered in the area, and the banknotes we have just recovered from your neighbours' property. You do not have to say anything. But it may harm your defence if you do not mention when questioned something which you later rely on in court. Anything you do say may be given in evidence."

She stared at him. "*What?*"

"Do you understand I have cautioned you regarding anything you say about the briefcase, and the money, recently found in the vicinity of your property, and which we believe you have played a part in taking or concealing?"

He thought he heard a snigger from the Geddeses' boundary, not far from where they stood. Amanda glared venomously towards her neighbour's. When she looked back at Ian, tears were trickling slowly down her cheeks. "I know *you'll* understand," she mumbled brokenly.

"Are you well enough to continue, Ms Finnes?" He was glad he had brought DC Rickshaw with him. If they were in for hysterics, he'd rather have a witness.

Amanda heaved a sob. But she nodded in response to his question, and when she spoke it was with seething anger. "It's *Terry's* doing!" She spat out the name, and the colour surged into her pale face. "It's all *his* fault!"

Through persistent questioning, her story emerged from disjointed pieces. Now and again, there was movement in the foliage at the Geddeses' boundary. Ian imagined Bob Geddes straining to hear what she was saying. Since they had moved to a greater distance from the boundary for privacy – and were now sat in deck chairs by her woodpile – there was no way Bob could hear, but he wasn't giving up.

They established that Terry Vass was Amanda Finnes' ex-boyfriend. He had used her and then left her, taking with him the five thousand pounds she had loaned him. Her anger and bitterness were obvious.

Now, enter Lisette Simmons into the tale. She had come on the scene about the time of Amanda's break-up with Terry. She had been so supportive; it was through Lisette that Amanda had discovered Terry's philandering ways and the fact that he had also been seeing Tanya Fletcher. Amanda thought that Lisette had also had a fling with Terry; how else would she know so much about him?

Ian asked, "What exactly does Lisette know about Terry?"

"Oh, just the type of man he was. She really got him. You know." She was attributing knowledge to him again – or more likely filling gaps with '*you know*' when she had no idea herself.

Amanda had begun watching Terry; Lisette watched him too. You know, at Molly's cottage, which they could see from the cover of Torrdara Forest.

"Did you watch him together?"

No, not together – they *talked* about it together, and Amanda always felt Lisette must have watched Terry as she seemed to know when Terry was at the cottage. Amanda was enjoying the account now. The tears had dried up; the threat of hysterics had passed. She was flattered with the interest both detectives showed; she seemed to have forgotten how many crimes she might have committed.

One day, Amanda saw Terry from her hiding place in the forest. He went to the usual shed; yes, he used one for storage; there was a new padlock on the door so she thought it must be important to him.

Ian asked, "Do you know anything about the reporting of a strange man close to Mrs Johnson's cottage?"

"That was me! I thought it might get Terry into trouble," Amanda said eagerly. "And I thought the police should be informed," she added as an afterthought.

"I see." Ian's dry tone was lost on her.

There wasn't much more to her account. If she was to be believed, Amanda had waited until Terry had gone and opened the padlock on the shed door by cracking the combination lock. "It's not that difficult," she said. "I bought myself a similar lock from Amazon and practised bypassing the code by watching YouTube. In fact, I think I can do it better than the YouTube tutorials. I ought to start my own channel!"

"I'd stick to your day job if I were you," remarked Ian, and Amanda giggled.

She had acted on impulse when she removed the case (which she admitted struggling with because of its weight) and took the route through Hangman's Wood back to her house. No, she wasn't concerned that Molly would see or hear her; she knew Molly was nearly always snoozing in her chair, with the TV on full volume. Hidden in Hangman's Wood, Amanda managed to get into the case (cracking another couple of combination locks), removed the money she was owed (plus an undisclosed amount she *didn't* mention to Ian), reset the locks, and then spotted Cath Geddes in her back garden. Since she hadn't really got a plan where to keep the case, and since she feared Terry might come after her, she asked Cath to look after it – until she could decide what to do.

"So Lisette wasn't part of this?"

"Oh no! That was all me," Amanda said proudly. "In fact, Lisette was annoyed that I involved Cath – I think she thought *she* should have had the case! She was always trying to take over. She thinks I'm stupid – I think she was surprised that I managed so much on my own! Anyway, I thought that if Terry knew Lisette too, he might go after her when he found his precious money was missing."

"So, you gave it to your *neighbour* to hide?" Ian didn't disguise his incredulity.

She shrugged. "As I say, I didn't plan it, I just thought that Terry wasn't likely to think of it being taken by an older couple he didn't even know! It was all done so suddenly – and I never dreamt Molly would die and Cath wouldn't give it back!"

It was like a far-fetched mystery, featuring one – or two – women obsessed with getting comeuppance on Terry Vass. Yet, it fit with the Geddeses' account, and they appeared to have zero motive to collude with their now-detested neighbour.

Amanda freely admitted that she had also made the phone call to the Crimestoppers number about stolen money stored in Cath Geddes' garage. She seemed pleased, not sorry, with this stroke of genius. "Cath messed up our plans," she said. "She wouldn't give it back! I didn't see why *they* should keep it when it was *me* – and Lisette – that Terry might come after!"

If Ian felt sorry for anyone in this whole debacle, it was Cath Geddes. They had duped her into helping them, dumped the money on her, and expected her to play along with their whims. Cath admitted she had overheard the women in Hangman's Wood – which explained the odd CCTV footage of her lying down in the forest. Ian could imagine her feelings on discovering how she had been used. *No wonder she didn't return the briefcase!* Amanda didn't seem to feel there would be any comeback for her part in using her neighbours, but Ian wasn't so sure he'd like to live next door to Bob Geddes after doing what *she'd* done. Apart from possible criminal charges, there would almost certainly be repercussions in the future.

As if reading his mind, Amanda asked, "Will I be charged with anything?"

What a nightmare for a prosecutor! Any lawyer worth his salt would paint Amanda as Terry Vass' victim – used and abused and only trying to get from him the money she was owed. The Crown Office wasn't likely to pursue serious charges, but he wasn't going to tell Amanda that yet. Instead, he mentioned the various crimes which could be laid at her door – handling and concealing stolen goods, wasting police time, perpetrating deception on neighbours, arguably for personal gain, which could be criminal fraud, and possibly other offences. "We'll be taking advice regarding charges which could be brought against you," he concluded.

He had half expected hysterics, but he was mistaken. She seemed to regard criminal charges as unlikely; *she was a victim too, wasn't she?* She actually *winked at him,* as if they shared a secret understanding, as if he was on *her* side. Ian got to his feet, bringing the interview to an abrupt end. He had no idea at what point he had earned her approbation; he certainly didn't care for it. He collected the remainder of the five thousand pounds she had admitted to claiming from the briefcase and she watched while he put it in a plastic bag, not seeming quite as concerned as he thought she might.

"Well, one good thing has come from this," she said, as she rushed to catch up with his quick strides away.

"Surprise me," he said sardonically.

"You don't think I'm serious," she said playfully. "But I'll tell you. The novel I'm writing – the one I told you about before – well, all this has inspired me!"

"Really."

He found her attitude rather disgusting. Beneath the mouth curved into that perpetual smile was a malevolence which was all the more startling because it was so well hidden. He had thought her a little unstable, easily duped, perhaps vulnerable, definitely anxious: but not *this.*

"I'll send you a copy of my book when it's finished." She laughed. "You might even find that you star in it!"

CHAPTER 23

Tuesday 12 May 2020 continued

While Lisette made a final phone call, Ken packed the car. There were surprisingly few personal effects – but plenty of electronic equipment. Besides which, he had to leave space for the ridiculously large dog Lisette had borrowed from a friend. She said it was to help her blend in and get to know the locals, but since the animal never did anything she said, Ken thought Monty a hazard more than a help.

"What about the camera at the cottage?" Ken asked as she joined him.

She shook her head. "We don't have time. It's out of commission now anyway and likely won't be discovered for years."

As they turned left onto the road towards Kinbackie and main travel routes, she saw DS Prentice's car coming from Amanda Finnes' driveway, perhaps heading for *her*.

"It's a shame we weren't able to bring Terry on board," she said. "I still think he would have talked. For a price."

Ken yawned. "Not for lack of trying. You'd think we'd have learnt more once you'd cloned his phone."

She shook her head. "He was more careful than we gave him credit for. Besides, I expect he mostly used burner phones. We probably brought Terry's *career* – such as it is – if not his *life* to a premature end. I wouldn't want to be in his shoes explaining where the money is!" She adjusted the rear-view mirror, watching for any sign of the detective's car.

"But at least we stopped the payment. In a roundabout way!" Ken chuckled. "This one certainly had its twists and turns! Your face when we spotted Amanda taking the briefcase from that shed!"

It was not a happy memory and Lisette's scowl told Ken that he had pushed far enough recalling the more entertaining (in his opinion) aspects of the case.

On a more positive note, he commented, "It's amazing she never suspected how you *happened* to come across her when she was giving the case to Cath Geddes!"

"But not soon enough to stop it happening!" Lisette waved and smiled at an older couple walking their dog along the road. Two sets of eyes swivelled and followed the car's progress. It was impossible to hide the overfull car; they looked as if they were going on holiday during lockdown.

"Friends of yours?" asked Ken.

"Can't remember their names. I wonder what the locals will make of our sudden disappearance!"

Ken yawned again. "Sorry, boss! Night shift watching Scottish wildlife isn't my idea of fun!"

She chuckled. "What triggered the motion detector last night?"

"An owl of some kind and two badgers."

"*Two!*"

He smiled wryly at her sarcastic tone. "But no sign of Terry's boss, whoever he really is."

"Or *she*."

"You still think it's possible that crazy woman Amanda could be a high-ranking narcotrafficker linked to an OCG[5]…?"

---

[5] OCG – Organised Crime Group

She shook her head. "I don't know – but she isn't what she seemed. After seeing her constantly for weeks, she was still inconsistent and unpredictable, frankly a bit crazy…"

"Taking the money from under our noses!" Ken chuckled.

Lisette was not amused. "Perhaps she was keeping an eye on that money right under our noses! She might have been a very clever actress!"

"But to involve the Geddeses? High risk if not really stupid strategy!"

"I know, I know. It doesn't make sense to suspect her, and yet … Well, anyway, it was a long shot that we'd learn the identity of the local drug lord as well as intercept the payment for the next shipment … You don't happen to know where the nearest coffee stop is?"

Ken shook his head and reclined his car seat. "Don't wake me if you find one. You OK to drive to the border, boss?

"Doesn't look like I've got much choice!"

"Wake me when we get there." Ken shut his eyes. He'd spent several weeks hiding out in the backend of nowhere, with stupid badgers and other wildlife constantly setting off the motion sensor of the camera any hour of the day and night, sending him rushing to his monitor only to see them wandering aimlessly across his line of vision as if mocking him; add to that taking directions from his loud-mouthed boss 24/7 … but it had had its reward after all. Once more, he carefully traced the chain of evidence before he succumbed to sleep. Was there *any* possibility that the wad of cash, *one hundred thousand pounds*, could be traced to *him*? Who would believe blundering Bob Geddes' account that he had returned it? At worst, it would be Bob Geddes' word against his. There was no one else who knew.

When the motion alarm was triggered at the crack of dawn on Sunday morning, he'd dutifully dragged himself from bed and checked the monitor, expecting to see an animal. Instead, he'd spotted Bob Geddes returning the briefcase. He'd rushed down to the shed, never dreaming what he'd find; he nabbed the hundred grand bundle and returned to bed; his boss had never even stirred. He ensured there was no camera footage of him at the shed; the money was long gone by the time Amanda and Lisette went to the cottage to return the loose notes from Amanda Finnes' driveway and find the scribbled note.

He alone had seen all the camera footage; ultimately, he controlled what remained recorded and archived. Most of the images of wildlife in the forest clearing would be deleted. No, there was no real danger. He was the invisible lackey, the boring techie. But he deserved every penny of his prize. He slipped into sleep with an easy mind.

CHAPTER 24

Wednesday 13 May 2020 – Wednesday 20 May 2020

Ian read the autopsy report again. When he had discovered that the fingerprints taken from Tanya Fletcher's house belonged to Terry Vass, he wondered whether there was foul play in her death. In fact, with possible links to the NCA case, and the knowledge that Tanya Fletcher had transferred three thousand pounds to an account in the name of – yes, *Terry Vass* – Ian half expected it.

But that wasn't what he was looking at. Tanya Fletcher's likely cause of death was a *subarachnoid haemorrhage* – a sudden stroke, caused by bleeding into the space around the brain. Yes, it was unusual; but it wasn't impossible, or, it seemed, suspicious. Her National Health Service medical records showed no previous reported symptoms; aside from the possibility of a sudden severe headache, Ms Fletcher probably lost consciousness not knowing she would never wake again. In addition, Tanya Fletcher had tested positive for Covid-19. As so much remained unknown about the new virus there were questions around whether Tanya had suffered complications which contributed to the haemorrhage. Either way, with no other evidence, her death was not felt to be suspicious.

It seemed that Tanya had been estranged from her family, but at last her sister, who lived in Aberlochee, had come forward to take care of arrangements; any other details about the woman, how she came to be so alone, and how she was connected to a man like Terry Vass, would probably never be known.

That week saw the end of the NCA case – at least so far as the northern police force were concerned. Examination of the broken briefcase which once contained the money, and of the notes which had been dug up from Bob and Cath's hiding place in Hangman's Wood, verified both as being associated with the NCA case. In total, just over eight hundred and eighty-eight thousand pounds was recovered. The case and the banknotes were dispatched by police courier to the NCA.

Ian's part in proceedings was over but felt frustratingly *unfinished*. He thought of the thick forest behind the homes which were primarily involved in finding (or storing) the money. Over one hundred thousand pounds remained missing. Had Bob and Cath kept a separate stash of notes buried in another hiding place in the wood? Or had Bob told the truth about leaving an untouched bundle of notes – one hundred thousand pounds – in the case when he left it at Molly Johnson's cottage? In which case, who had taken it? Terry Vass? Amanda Finnes? Lisette Simmons?

Lisette Simmons was a slippery customer if ever there was one. He instinctively felt she was hiding something, and after listening to Amanda's account, which implicated Lisette in knowing a great deal more than she had admitted to, he felt that she was at the core of the business. The fact that she had vanished just before he had arrived to question her only heightened his suspicions.

Wherever the remaining missing banknotes were, and whatever game Lisette Simmons had played, it was unfortunately not worth expending police resources in further discovery. The missing notes' serial numbers were logged on the police system; if they entered the world of commerce another way – such as through a shop or a bank, they would probably never be found.

AFTERWARDS

Summer 2020

Bob and Cath weren't charged with receiving stolen goods. No matter how much they would like to have profited from the money, and certainly would have done had there been opportunity, there were far too many extenuating circumstances for the Crown Office to build a case. The couple were left in peace – at least so far as the law was concerned. Peace did *not* pervade their lives or neighbourhood for long with their nemesis living next door.

Amanda had received a Recorded Police Warning for her part in the money debacle. Ian felt she deserved a lot more than that, but the Crown Office wasn't keen on any active prosecution against her. A Recorded Police Warning was the least – and turned out to be the most – that Ian could reward her for her actions.

Soon the file occupied by the neighbour dispute of Finnes and Geddes began to figuratively bulge at the seams. Ian was thankful it didn't fall under his purview; from curiosity he occasionally enquired what the latest accusation and counteraccusation was. Investigations of harassment, breach of the peace, trespass, and even assault were duly investigated and were generally a waste of police time; nothing was proven.

When he heard that Amanda Finnes' small dog died, he was sorry for her. The Geddeses' were blamed for poisoning it; another page was added to the file.

***

It was late summer, when Molly Johnson's cottage had finally been cleared and was being assessed for renovation, that Colonel Urquhart called Ian. "There's something here you might want to see," he said.

On a tree opposite the shed that Terry Vass had been so interested in, there had been a bird nesting box – which had been knocked down by a freak branch in recent wind. Inside the nesting box was a tiny camera – to be precise, a high-tech, Zeamitz 220 Wireless Camera. It wasn't live, but Ian would have bet a fair bit that it had been for those crazy couple of weeks back in April and May. *Someone* had watched all the comings and goings to the storage place which once contained one million pounds. *Someone* had probably spotted him and the Colonel there the afternoon they had visited the cottage together. If it was Terry Vass, no wonder he hadn't returned. He would have known not to. Ian took the camera back to the station.

On little more than a hunch, he searched for the camera's serial number on the *Police Inventory Tracking and Recording Database*. The camera was listed. It was flagged 'Out of Action' and 'No Return'. It had been assigned to the NCA.

His boss made some phone calls.

"They were NCA officers, weren't they?" pressed Ian.

DI White nodded. "They claim they were about to inform us. Nice of them to remember! But yes, they had two officers on the ground – who have just finished a connected undercover assignment elsewhere – hence them not revealing their identity sooner. Or so they say. They hoped to turn Terry Vass and infiltrate an OCG – but they lost track of him. I can't imagine a happy ending for him since he lost the money due to pay for a shipment of drugs. The positive outcome is that none of the cash reached its intended destination – and the shipment of drugs they were tracking via the Faroe Islands to mainland Scotland were seized on arrival. A few arrests, but no one of significance as far as I know."

"I don't suppose they'd share their camera footage of the shed they were watching?"

"You suppose correctly! But what would be the point now?"

Ian shrugged slightly. "Curiosity – and a missing hundred grand. Did the NCA officers recover any more of the money?"

The DI nodded. "Just under five thousand in loose one-hundred notes, I believe."

Ian shook his head. *Who to believe?* It still revolved around the three women. Cath Geddes, aided most ably by her husband Bob, could have hidden the final missing bundle of cash in the wood in a separate hiding place. Amanda Finnes could have removed it from the briefcase before she gave it into Cath's keeping, or once it was returned to the shed; perhaps she had continued spying on Terry Vass and spotted Bob returning the case instead? Lisette Simmons could have found far more than was returned to the NCA; had she awarded herself a nice fat paycheque?

Whatever the truth, with the evidence in other hands, he would never know.

***

Autumn 2020

As the coronavirus pandemic once more fastened its grip on the world, and restrictions began to tighten, the *Aberlochee Chronicle* reported that the body of a local man had been discovered 'in suspicious circumstances'. Which was an understatement. In fact, what was not disclosed was that he had been shot through the back of the head at point-blank range.

"Well, I never!" remarked Bob. "Caff, guess what happened to that chap called Terry Vass? ... TURN THE TELLY DOWN, CAFF! ... I said, TERRY VASS! ... The one the WOMEN WERE MIXED UP WITH! Well, anyway, poor blighter's dead! ... No, it doesn't say HOW, but I reckon those women got him before he could get them! Where're you off to, then?"

"Out."

"I can see that! It's raining!"

"I'm taking Cable round the wood. You could start peeling the potatoes." She didn't wait for an answer. Cable came running, and, slipping the leash on his collar, she fastened her jacket and stepped into the rain.

Torrdara Forest offered some shelter from the penetrating damp. She waved as Emily approached with her dog, Peter. They knew each other's timing and had met by arrangement a few times now. They still held diametrically opposed worldviews, but Cath enjoyed their chats.

As they began to follow the damp forest path, Cath asked, "Did you ever know someone called Terry Vass?"

Emily shook her head. "I don't think so, was he a local man?"

"There's quite a story." Cath pointed to a thicket of trees, behind which *Cois Dara* was screened. "You never knew anything about the money found there?"

"No!" Emily was clearly intrigued. "Well, I found a hundred-pound note, as you know, and the detective on the case told me it was from a hoard of stolen money, and I heard rumours – which you can't really avoid – about the old cottage being involved…"

"Elspeth, of course."

"Yes – but I took the story of a crime group or drug cartel operating in the area with a pinch of salt."

Cath remarked, "I think Terry Vass was a local crime boss, or drug lord, or whatever they call such people these days."

"In Strathavie?!"

"It does seem unlikely, doesn't it?" Cath agreed. Although Emily had never asked about their part in the saga, she *must* have heard a version of events which mentioned the Geddeses. Cath told the story; she didn't bother to hide her anger with Amanda and Lisette; of Lisette she said, "She disappeared, so I think she was one of the drug gang"; she even described her own thoughts about whether it was right or wrong to keep the money. She concluded with the news she had just heard. Terry Vass was dead. "But apart from breaking the law, if there is no God – no invisible judge or anything of that sort – whatever any of us did wouldn't be wrong, as such. Even keeping Molly's money if she'd been alive and needed it, in fact, even stealing it from her wouldn't actually be *wrong*, would it? If you're not caught, there's nothing to worry about."

"No," Emily agreed. "But I'm glad I don't live in a world like *that.*"

"Would there really be any difference?" Cath looked sideways at her.

"In a world full of people without a personal conscience about anything? I can't imagine anything worse! What would any of us *not* do to better ourselves if we thought there was no one to see or hold us accountable?"

Cath shook her head. "Well, personally, I don't want God judging me! I don't mind God being there if He's going to let me in to heaven one day, but if He's going to judge us all, then, frankly, we're all going to hell!"

"Yes," agreed Emily, and Cath stared at her in surprise.

"You think *you're* going to hell too?"

"Unless there's a way of being right with God again, of having our sins forgiven, then yes, we all are. Whether in big or small ways we have all broken our Creator's laws, so we all deserve His punishment."

"Then we'd both better hope God *isn't* true!" retorted Cath.

"Unless there *is* a way to be forgiven and made right with God again."

Cath smiled sardonically. "And you think there is, of course."

Emily nodded. "A plan made by God Himself to completely wipe the slate clean."

"Religion of some sort, I presume?"

"No! The last thing we need is a set of rules or rituals. We need a Saviour, a mediator to stand between us and God and put things right for us."

"Ah, is this where Jesus comes in? I wondered when we'd get to Him."

"It's all about Him. God sent His Son, Jesus Christ, to be the Saviour of the world. If we personally choose to accept what He did on our behalf, when He died on the cross to bear the punishment for our sins, then our sins are forgiven, and we're made right with God again. But the decision rests with us."

Cath kicked the tennis ball that Peter, unsuccessful in gaining Emily's attention, suddenly flung at her feet. Overhead, a bird flew swiftly through the trees. Nearby, a tiny Jenny Wren chattered from thick undergrowth. At last, Cath commented, "It's a pretty simplistic solution, though. Just trust in God and tell Him you accept what Jesus did? It sounds too easy!"

Emily pulled up the hood on her jacket as the rain grew heavier. "You think it's easy? In one way it is, I suppose – it's something everyone can understand; but think how difficult it is to give up all our notions of how good we are, our own ideas of what is right and wrong, our own treasured version of 'truth' that we've cultivated to suit ourselves – to admit that we're wrong and that God is right; to accept that Jesus Christ is the only way back to God. It will cost us all our pride. Is that *easy?*"

It was obvious that Emily herself was perfectly sincere in her belief. "Well, it's good you've found something that makes you happy," Cath said. "At the end of the day, that's all we can do."

Déjà vu. Emily remembered a similar comment in a previous discussion. "What have you found that makes you happy?" she asked.

"Oh, pleasing ourselves, good living, doing our best, you know. Bob and I never had much time for *religion* – no offence. Life's complicated enough without adding *God* into it!"

"But what is left *without* Him?"

The words echoed in Cath's mind after they parted and she and Cable continued their solitary walk around the forest track. *What was left without God?*

Blind, pitiless indifference. That's what.

***

As the leaves began to fall in earnest and the damp mists of late autumn shrouded Strathavie, Ian received an unexpected email.

Amanda Finnes informed him that she had moved location (which explained why the neighbour nuisance complaints had ceased). She thanked him for his special kindness to her (which astonished him) and attached a link to her self-published novel. She referred to their invisible connection ('*I know you understand me*') and said that she hoped she had *done him justice* in the book.

With significant misgivings, he downloaded the ebook and flicked through it. So far as he could tell, it was a farfetched mystery about missing money. The heroine was a sensitive, psychic woman who solved the case and located the cash through her astonishing powers of supernatural perception.

No surprises there. She may as well have called the heroine by her own name.

The villains were the neighbours, who died grizzly deaths which she had foreseen and of which she had tried (*'with kindness they did not deserve'*) to warn them … *'their bodies bloated and rotting in the cursed wood'*. The hero … *a young, handsome, swarthy police officer,* who fell hopelessly in love with the heroine…

Ian could only imagine the ribbing he would receive should this ghastly fiction ever come to light. Fervently hoping that it wouldn't, against all conceivable odds, turn into a bestseller that any of his friends or colleagues might read, he deleted the file.

Unknown to him, Amanda spent several thousand pounds publishing the book in print and audiobook formats and on extensive advertising. Until the additional funds she had taken from Terry Vass' briefcase (as 'compensation' for the emotional damage he had caused her), dried up.

Thankfully for Ian, the book still flopped.

***

There may still be stray one-hundred-pound Scottish banknotes lost in the wilds of Strathavie

DISCLAIMER & END MATTERS

This novella is a work of fiction. It is not intended to accurately portray matters of police, banking or any other procedure described in this book. Whilst some of the information I have used is factually correct, I have fabricated many details solely to suit the purposes of this imaginary story. Likewise, Strathavie and other named places are fictitious, and none of the characters in this story are real.

However, there is a serious point which I hold to be true. This relates to the Bible's answers to the most important questions of life: Where did we come from? Why are we here? What is the purpose of life? Is there such a thing as good and evil? Is God real? Is there life after death? And so on. If you've never considered Biblical answers to these questions or have assumed that the Bible doesn't offer evidence-based answers to these issues, I hope you are challenged to explore what the Bible has to say about them. Apart from reading the Bible itself, there are plenty of other resources available.

Among others, John Lennox, Emeritus Professor of Mathematics at the University of Oxford, has written and spoken widely on these subjects, including in debate with Professor Richard Dawkins. His books are widely available, and you can watch his debates on YouTube. [https://www.johnlennox.org]

William Lane Craig, Professor of Philosophy, has also written and spoken widely on these issues – you can find his debates on YouTube and listen to his podcast.
[https://www.reasonablefaith.org]

There are many more.

For more books by Eunice Wilkie, please visit:
www.aletheiabooks.co

Printed in Great Britain
by Amazon